D0729313

Phantom Stallion

The Wild One

TERRI FARLEY

SCHOLASTIC INC.

New York Toronto London Auckland Sydney
Mexico City New Delhi Hong Kong Buenos Aires

No part of this publication may be reproduced in whole or in part,
or stored in a retrieval system, or transmitted in any form or by any means,
electronic, mechanical, photocopying, recording, or otherwise,
without written permission of the publisher.
For information regarding permission, write to HarperCollins Children's Books,
a division of HarperCollins Publishers, 1350 Avenue of the Americas, New York, NY 10019.

ISBN 0-439-58492-2

Copyright © 2002 by Terri Sprenger-Farley.
All rights reserved.
Published by Scholastic Inc., 557 Broadway, New York, NY 10012,
by arrangement with HarperCollins Children's Books, a division of HarperCollins Publishers.
SCHOLASTIC and associated logos are trademarks and/or registered trademarks of Scholastic Inc.

12 11 10 9 8 7 6 5 4 3 2 1   3 4 5 6 7 8/0

Printed in the U.S.A.   40

First Scholastic printing, September 2003

This book is dedicated to
Barbara and Bob Sprenger,
who let me talk to horses

Acknowledgments

Many people helped turn *Phantom Stallion* from a dream into a book. Dawn Lappin, Linda Dufurrena, C.J. Hadley, Maxine Shane, Tom Seley, and Bryan Fuell provided inspiration and expertise. Karen Solem, Julia Richardson, Elise Howard, Abby McAden, and Amanda Maciel "saw" my phantom stallion and believed in him. Chris Platt was my tireless critique partner. C.C. Ramirez shared her library skills at a moment's notice. Dave Moore, editor deluxe, gave me assignments that made me saddle sore and happy. Most of all, I'm thankful for Kate, Matt, and Cory, who gave me their patience, laughter, and love.

I hope Adalaide Bland's angel is smiling. Like all good teachers, she knew drawing horses on homework wouldn't keep me from learning.

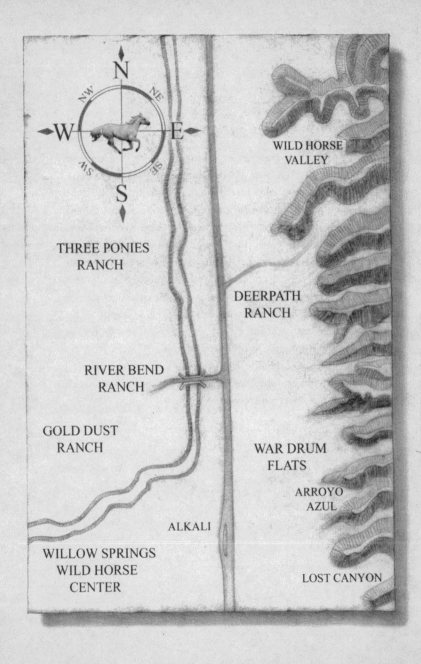

Chapter One ✑

At FIRST, SAM THOUGHT she was seeing things. The windshield of Dad's truck was pitted by years of windblown dust. Maybe she'd been away from the ranch so long, the desert sun was playing tricks on her eyes.

Suddenly, she knew better.

Mustangs stampeded over the ridge top. They ran down the steep hillside. As their hooves touched level ground, a helicopter bobbed up behind them.

It hovered like a giant dragonfly.

As she watched the herd, Sam saw one creamy mane flickering amid the dark necks of the other horses. She saw a black horse shining like glass and two roans running side by side. Here and there ran foals, nostrils wide with effort.

Sam wondered if the men hovering above could see each running horse, or only a flowing mass of animals.

The mustangs ran for the open range. Sam knew the horses would find little shade and less water ahead, but they seemed to think of nothing except outrunning the men and their machine.

The herd swung left. The helicopter swooped, ten feet off the sand, to block them.

The herd galloped right. With a whirring sound, the helicopter followed.

Then, from the back of the herd, a silver stallion raced forward. Sam never imagined a horse could be so beautiful, but there he was. He nipped and screamed, turning the mares in a wide U back under the helicopter's belly, running back to the hills and safety.

The helicopter pulled up. It banked into a turn and followed, but it was too late.

"Wow! Where did they go?" Sam's thigh muscles tensed. She sat inside her dad's truck, but her knees shook as if she'd been running with the wild horses.

"Mustangs have their secret getaway trails. They go places even a chopper can't." Dad took one hand off the steering wheel to pull his Stetson down to shade his eyes.

Sam cleared her throat and looked out the window at dull, brown Nevada. Could she have felt homesick for this?

Yes. Every day of the past two years, an ache had grown under her breastbone.

She just wished Dad would talk more. She wanted to hear about the ranch and the horses and Gram. But the nearer they got to the ranch, the more he acted like the dad she remembered. Relaxed and quiet, he was completely *un*like the awkward man who'd come to visit in Aunt Sue's polished San Francisco apartment.

Since he'd picked Sam up—literally off her feet in the middle of the airport—their conversation had bumped along just like this old truck. Slow, but sure.

"Shouldn't use helicopters and trucks," Dad muttered. "They just don't savvy mustangs."

Translated, that meant he had no respect for men who didn't understand the wild horses they were capturing and taking off the range.

Dad really talked like a cowboy. And his first name was Wyatt, a cowboy name if she'd ever heard one. Plus, he walked with the stiff grace of a man who'd ridden all his life.

When he'd first sent her to the city, Sam had been so angry, she'd tried to forget Dad. For a while, it had been easy.

After her accident, the doctors had said Sam might suffer "complications." When a girl fell from a galloping horse and her head was struck by a hoof, that was bad. When she lost consciousness as well, they explained, it was far worse.

Fear made Dad agree to send Sam away from the ranch, to live with Aunt Sue. In San Francisco, she was only two minutes away from a hospital, instead of two hours.

First Sam had begged to stay, then she'd turned stubborn and refused to go. But Dad was just as stubborn. He wouldn't take no for an answer. Since she'd barely turned eleven, Dad had won.

After a few lonely weeks, she'd learned to love San Francisco. Aunt Sue's willingness to take her everywhere and show her everything eased the pain of leaving home, but it couldn't make her forget Blackie.

Blackie had been the first horse who was all her own. She'd raised him through a rocky colthood, gentled him to accept her as his rider, then made a terrible mistake that injured her and frightened him into escape.

Each time Dad called her in San Francisco, Sam asked for word of Blackie. But the swift two-year-old had vanished.

In time, Sam stopped asking. She and Blackie had hurt each other. She'd been unable to go after him and touch him and explain. So, Blackie had followed his mustang heart back to the wild country.

Although Aunt Sue didn't ride, she did share Sam's passion for movies. Sam made friends at her middle school, too, and played basketball in a YMCA league. It wasn't long before the months had added up to two years.

Still, movies and basketball couldn't measure up

to Sam's memories of riding the range, fast and free. Sam never stopped loving horses and missing them. When Dad announced it was safe to come home, Sam had started packing.

Now, Sam sneaked another look at Dad. In San Francisco, she'd been embarrassed by him. She'd worried that her city friends would hear his buckaroo slang, or take a good look at his face, all brown and lean as beef jerky. If they had, they would have known Dad for what he was: a cowboy.

But here in Nevada, he fit in and it was easier for her to see she had a lot in common with him. They were both skinny, tanned, and stubborn.

"You really liked living in San Francisco?" Dad asked.

"After I got used to the fog and traffic, I loved it. I jogged in Golden Gate Park with Aunt Sue and we saw at least three movies every weekend."

Dad glanced her way with eyes as cold as a Hollywood gunfighter's. He hated the city.

Sam shrugged as if she didn't care. If he'd left the ranch more often to visit her, this wouldn't be so awkward. She and Dad might have a lot in common, but when he asked questions like that, hard-eyed and expecting a certain answer, Sam felt like a stranger.

She crossed one knee over the other and jiggled her foot. She ignored Dad's frown, which said he was disappointed that his daughter had become such a city slicker.

"Not far to River Bend, now," Dad said.

As if she didn't know they were near the ranch. She couldn't wait to see if it was the horse paradise she remembered. She only hoped she could still ride like she had before the accident.

She remembered so little of that moment. Falling. Breathing dust. Impact just over her right ear. The sound of Blackie's hooves galloping away, fading, gone. The accident wouldn't keep her from riding, because she wasn't afraid. She *wasn't*.

Sam fanned herself, wishing she hadn't worn black jeans and a black tee shirt. What was fashionable in San Francisco might be considered weird in rural Nevada.

She blew her bangs out of her eyes. Using Aunt Sue's sewing scissors, Sam had cut off her reddish-brown ponytail. She didn't want to look like the child Dad had sent away.

She straightened to look at herself in the truck's mirror. She'd accomplished her goal, all right. She didn't look like a little kid; she looked like a teenager with a bad haircut.

Sam shifted against her seat belt, stared out the truck's back window, and blinked.

Half-hidden in dust stood a horse. His powerful shoulders glittered in the sun, convincing her he was the silver stallion who'd turned the herd, but he had the dished face and flaring nostrils of an Arabian. She hadn't seen a horse that perfect since —

"Sam?" Dad's voice hit like a bucket of cold water. "What are you staring at, honey?"

Sam looked at Dad. Then, before she told him, Sam turned back around to make sure of what she'd seen.

"Uh, nothing," she said. The horse had disappeared. Had it been a mirage?

Never mind. In minutes she'd be at River Bend and she'd have a horse of her own, again.

Still, Sam couldn't help glancing back over her shoulder one last time. The first place she'd ride would be here, wherever *here* was, to find that ghost horse.

Sam saw a metallic glint against the sky. The helicopter was still searching.

Sam worried about the mustangs. Even a city girl knew how some cattle ranchers accused mustangs of eating all the grass and drinking water holes dry. A newspaper article she'd taken to class for Current Events had told how wild horses roaming Nevada's range were rounded up with government helicopters, then penned until they were adopted.

Sam remembered that half the girls in class had waved their hands over their heads, volunteering to take wild horses into their apartments or carports. Now here she was, with wild horses practically in her front yard.

"I can't wait to get you up on Ace," Dad nodded, smiling. Apparently he wasn't holding a grudge because she liked San Francisco. "You two are a match for sure."

Ace. Could there be a more perfect name for a cow pony? Sam had to smile. Dad said Ace "stuck to a calf like a burr on a sheep's tail." She supposed that meant Ace was a good cutting horse, able to separate the calves from the herd.

"I wish you had a picture of Ace."

Dad laughed. "And have him get conceited around the other horses? That'd mean trouble for sure."

Dad squinted through the windshield as a flashy tan Cadillac drove straight at them, honking.

"Speaking of trouble . . ." Dad shook his head and coasted to a stop.

"Who is it?" Sam tried to read Dad's face. "Don't you want to talk to him?"

"I'd rather take a shortcut over quicksand."

The Cadillac's window eased down, revealing the driver.

"Hey, Wyatt." The driver had slick hair and a toothpaste-commercial grin. His cowboy hat was as big as one of dad's truck tires. "This must be Samantha. Welcome, little lady."

No one called her Samantha—just Sam—but one thing Dad insisted upon was being courteous to adults. Sam smiled and wondered if she was supposed to recognize this guy.

"On your way to town?" Dad sounded neighborly, but his back looked stiff.

The man slumped back in his seat, all relaxed, and Sam nearly groaned. A horse of her own waited at the ranch. She wanted to see Ace, run her hands over his neck and smell the alfalfa sweetness of his soft nose. And this guy looked like he'd settled in for a long chat. When he lit a cigarette and threw his match on the desert floor, she knew she was right.

"Sam, this is Linc Slocum." Dad sighed.

"I'm your new neighbor, Samantha." He nodded. "Even though we've never met, I've heard lots of stories about you and that one-man horse of yours that escaped."

One-girl horse, Sam corrected silently. Blackie had bonded with her, because she'd used the Native American horse taming tricks her pal Jake Ely had taught her. She'd breathed into the colt's nostrils so he'd know her scent, she'd mounted him for the first time in water, and she'd called him by a secret name.

After the accident, lying in a hospital bed, Sam had worried that no one could call Blackie back. Her mind kept replaying the sound of his hooves galloping, then fading away, but she'd told no one the colt's secret name.

How could a stranger know Blackie had been a one-girl horse?

Dad's voice interrupted her memories. "Nice seein' you, Linc, but we'd better head on."

Even when Dad started to drive, Linc kept talking. That's when Sam knew Linc Slocum was no cowboy. Real cowboys hardly talked, even when they had something to say.

"If it hadn't been for that danged Jake—"

Confusion nipped at Sam's memory. She'd let *Jake* down, failing to ride Blackie right, but it sounded like Mr. Slocum blamed Jake for the accident.

Clearly, Dad didn't like Linc's implication.

Dad bumped his Stetson up from his brow and faced Linc Slocum head-on. Sam couldn't see Dad's expression, but Slocum pulled back like a turtle jerking his head in.

"Old news," Slocum said, but his smile slipped.

Sam shivered as if someone had sprinkled a handful of spiders down the neck of her shirt.

"Maybe he'll come home," Linc said.

Sam bit her lip. She knew better, but Dad's words still hurt.

"Don't get your hopes up," Dad said. "The wild ones never come back."

Chapter Two ⌒

$\mathcal{B}$OARDS RUMBLED UNDER Dad's tires as he crossed the bridge over the water that gave River Bend Ranch its name. Sam breathed the scent of sagebrush as they rolled under the tall wooden rectangle marking the ranch entrance.

A brown dog ran barking toward the truck.

"That's Blaze," Dad said. "He sleeps in the bunkhouse most of the time, but it looks like he's come to welcome you."

A cowboy yell split the summer silence.

Sam glanced left. She saw only a huge grassy pasture and horses grazing peacefully.

"Come on, now!" the same voice shouted again.

To her right, Sam saw the ranch house, white with green shutters. White curtains billowed from the upstairs window of her bedroom.

But all the racket was coming from a round corral, straight ahead.

As Dad pulled up next to the corral, Sam heard thudding hooves. She climbed down from the truck in time to see her old buddy Jake fly over a horse's buck-lowered head. Jake cartwheeled through the air and skidded to a stop on the seat of his jeans. Dust rolled around him.

Sam peered through the log fence rails, then planted one shoe on the lowest one and climbed until she saw over the top.

A sassy paint mare stamped and snorted in the corner. Her intelligent eyes studied the rider she'd thrown. Then she blew a whuffling breath through her lips.

Jake ignored the mare and looked toward Sam. The instant after she realized he'd turned handsome, Sam remembered how Jake used to trick her, tease her, and stare down his nose as if she were a lower life-form.

And she'd deserved every bit of bullying. Jake lived on the nearby Three Ponies Ranch and only put up with her because he liked riding. Jake was the youngest of six brothers. At home, the oldest boys had dibs on fun chores, like working horses. As the youngest, Jake would have to collect hens' eggs and mend wire fences. So he chose to ride over to River Bend each morning where Dad let him train young horses.

Something about Jake just brought out the pest in her. There he sat, bucked off before her very eyes.

Sam was usually speechless around cute guys, but she couldn't resist teasing him.

"Oh Jake, what's wrong?" Sam said in a singsong voice, like the little kid she'd been.

Dad slouched against the fence rails beside her and chuckled. "I'd say you just missed a good chance to keep your mouth shut, Sam."

Behind her a screen door closed. Hens scratched and cackled. The scent of cooking wafted on the wind.

When Jake stood up, he looked a lot older than sixteen. He was almost smiling as he whomped his cowboy hat against his leg, knocking off dust. Then he resettled it on the Indian black hair he'd pulled back with a leather shoelace.

"Indian black" wasn't just an expression. Jake Ely was half Shoshone.

"Well, if it ain't Samantha." Jake walked toward the fence. He wore chinks, fringed leather leg coverings like short chaps. "Still skinnier than a wet weasel, aren't you, Sam?"

How weird that Linc Slocum's respectful "little lady" made her bristle and Jake's insult made her laugh.

"Jake, you leave Sam alone 'til she's had a chance to catch her breath." Grandma Grace slipped around the side of the corral. She wore a denim skirt with a pale blue blouse. Sam noticed its pattern of little red hearts, just before a hug closed around her.

"Gram." Sam's throat felt tight, but she fought back tears. She didn't need to look like a wimp already.

Gram hadn't missed a week of writing to her in San Francisco. Almost all the news Sam received from the ranch came from Gram.

"Besides, Sam looks like a nice young lady. Not a weasel." Gram touched Sam's hair, reminding her of the mistake she'd made cutting it. "You'll see that for yourself, Jake, when you've showered up for dinner and washed the dust out of your eyes."

Calling the midday meal "dinner" instead of lunch was one more thing Sam had forgotten.

When Dad hefted her backpack and duffle bag, Sam wished he'd put them down. She could wait to get inside the house. She could wait to breathe the remembered smells of woodsmoke and coffee and to fling herself down on the patchwork-quilted bed she knew Gram had kept ready for her. She could *not* wait to see her horse.

"Where's Ace?" she blurted.

"Let me drop these inside and I'll show you." Dad shrugged the backpack higher up his shoulder and walked toward the house.

"You're givin' her Ace?" Jake shouted after Dad. "*Ace?*" Jake yelled again, but the screen door had slammed closed. "You gotta be kidding." Jake rubbed the back of his neck, then faced Sam. He looked her over for just a second too long. Then said,

"Ace's smarter than you and me put together."

"Then he and I ought to do just fine." Sam looked down at Blaze. Since the Border collie was begging her to rub his ears, she did.

"Yeah? You're quite some rider, are you, Zorro?"

Sam looked up. She thought Jake's eyes clouded with something like worry, but she must have misread his look. Jake's joke had been aimed at her black tee shirt, black jeans, and black sneakers.

"Excuse me." Sam placed a hand against her chest and pretended to apologize. "Guess I've been in civilization so long I just plumb ran out of cowboy duds."

She didn't mention she'd only ridden four times in two years, and all four times had been in a stable's riding ring. She sure didn't tell Jake he'd hit on the one thing she was really worried about.

"You kids knock it off," Dad said as he returned from the house. He sounded amused, though, not a bit mad.

"I was only telling Sam how glad I am to see her." Jake's arm circled Sam's shoulders. Although his voice brimmed with sarcasm, Sam felt a genuine warmth in Jake's hug.

This might turn into her best summer yet.

Ace was runty. Fourteen hands at best, he stood alone.

When Sam came to the fence, the other horses lifted their heads and swished their tails with faint interest. A little grass fell from their lips before they went back to grazing.

Not Ace. If a horse could put his hands on his hips and look as if he were asking "And what do *you* want?" that's exactly what Ace did.

His hide glowed a nice warm bay and he had neat white hind socks, but a scar made a long line of lighter hair on his neck.

"Ace!" Sam held out a hand and smooched to him.

For a heartbeat, Ace was a horse transformed. His tiny head tilted sideways. His back-cast ears pricked up, black tips curving in. He pranced forward with the fluid grace of a dressage horse—until he saw that Sam's hand was empty.

Ace planted all four legs with a stiffness, which showed he was insulted.

"Told you he was smart." Jake laughed.

"I wasn't trying to trick him!" Sam said. "I just wanted him to come over and let me rub his ears."

From the ranch house porch, Gram clanged something metal against a triangle. She *didn't* shout "Come and get it," but they all hurried in for lunch. Except for Sam.

She stalled, thinking Ace might come to her if the others left. She was wrong. Ace looked at her, shivered his skin as if shaking off a fly, and yawned.

Mashed potatoes sat next to a mound of green beans fragrant with onions and bacon. Dad plopped a slab of beef on Sam's plate. All this for lunch.

Sam glanced around the kitchen. White plastered walls and oak beams made it cozy and bright at the same time. She wondered about the cardboard boxes stacked against the wall.

"I know he doesn't look like much, Sam," Dad said. "But Ace is a great little horse."

Before she answered, Sam noticed Jake kept a sidelong glance aimed her way as he reached for a platter piled with biscuits.

"I'm sure he's super," Sam said.

It wasn't that she minded Ace's size. She was barely five feet tall, herself. She could mount a small horse more easily. But that scar. And his *attitude* . . .

"What about that mark on his neck?"

"The freeze brand?" Jake held his butter knife in midair, and Sam knew she'd surprised him.

Sam looked from Jake to her father.

"That's what it is," Dad agreed. "Ace is a mustang. He used to run with the herd you saw today."

Gram made a hum of disapproval, but Sam didn't try to decipher it.

"After wild horses are rounded up and vaccinated, they're branded with liquid nitrogen," Dad explained. "That freezes the skin temporarily, the horse's fur turns white and—"

"Really? He was wild?" Sam's mind replayed the gelding's attitude. Ace hadn't been rude. He just had pride.

A stab of disloyalty deflated Sam's excitement as she remembered her lost colt.

"I wonder if he could've known—" Sam hesitated. "If he could've run with Blackie."

"That's a fool thing to say." Jake rocked his chair onto its back legs.

"It's not, is it?" Sam appealed to her father.

Dad blew his cheeks full of air and shook his head.

"Jake, put all four chair legs back on the floor, if you please," Gram ordered.

Jake's chair slammed down, but his face was flushed crimson. Did he hate her for losing the horse they'd worked so hard to train? Or did Jake's blush mean what Linc Slocum had implied: some folks blamed Jake for Sam's injury?

It didn't matter. The accident had happened years ago. She wanted to know where Blackie was *now*.

"What about that stallion we saw turning the herd away from the helicopter?" Sam's hands curled into fists. She kept them in her lap. "That was the Phantom, right? What if Blackie's running with the Phantom?"

Were they just going to let her babble until she ran out of breath?

"Now, Sam, first off, there's no such thing as the Phantom. There's been a white stud on this range as far back as I can recall. Dallas—you remember Dal, our foreman?"

Sam nodded, but her fists tightened with impatience.

"Well, he claims sometimes, when he's up late playing the guitar in front of the bunkhouse, he's seen a shadowy horse just across the river. He thinks it's the Phantom, drawn by the music." Dad shrugged, but Sam felt chills at the picture his words painted.

"Folks always call him the Phantom. But it's not the same horse year after year. He's a . . ." Dad put down his fork and rotated one hand in the air. "You know, like a local legend."

I know that, Sam wanted to interrupt, but Dad was trying to be nice, so she just listened.

"There's fast blood in one line of light-colored mustangs, that's all," Dad continued. "They haven't been caught because they run the legs off our saddle stock. Not because they're 'phantoms.'"

"But aren't white horses unusual? I mean, maybe it *is* the same horse. Maybe he's really old." Sam cut a green bean into four neat sections.

"Remember Smoke, Blackie's sire?" Dad asked. "That old cow pony was a mustang and he was dark as Blackie when he was a yearling. He turned gray by age five, but he was snow white by the time he died last spring.

"That's the way it is with most white horses, if they're not albinos, and that's all there is to this Phantom."

So quick that it startled them all, Gram stood up. She lifted the coffeepot, poured a cup for Dad, and set it before him.

"Who wants dessert?" Gram went to the counter and came back with a pie. She placed it on the table.

"I don't know." Sam wondered if she could eat another bite.

"No excuses, young lady." Gram's thick-bladed knife split the golden crust. She served Sam along with everyone else.

"And second, Sam," Dad watched her over the top of his coffee cup, "we've watched for your colt and haven't seen him. With all the trouble these horses are into—"

"And Linc bein' loco to catch the Phantom," Jake added.

"What he thinks he'll do with that stud is beyond me," Dad said, shaking his head.

"Wyatt, it's clear as glass what he intends." Gram sat down with her own pie. "Linc Slocum moved out West to play cowboy. He bought a ranch. He hired men to teach him to ride and rope. He bought clothes to look the part of a working buckaroo, but he only looks like he's wearing a costume.

"Folks still see him as an outsider," Gram said, mostly to Sam. "So he wants a wild white stallion that stands for everything he *can't* buy."

"Capturing the Phantom won't change what folks

think of him," Jake said.

"And it'll land him in jail if the Bureau of Land Management finds out," Dad added.

Sam fidgeted with her napkin. Linc Slocum gave her the creeps.

"If Blackie joined a herd headed away from here, it would be for his own good," Dad said, then swallowed his last bite of pie.

Sam thought for a minute, counting up the years. Blackie would be almost five by now. A stallion. With his mustang bloodlines, he could survive in the wild.

"Blackie's got a herd of his own, now," she said and crossed her arms. "That's what I think."

By the time Sam left the table, the snap on her jeans was pushing against her stomach. She felt stuffed and a little sleepy, but she could hardly wait to go ride Ace. Still, she tried to be polite.

"Want me to wash dishes?" she offered, then crossed her fingers. Please let Gram refuse.

"No, you better go try out your horse." Gram stacked the dishes.

Sam knew it wasn't fair to leave Gram indoors, while she, Dad, and Jake escaped into the June afternoon.

"Maybe I'll unpack first." Sam fidgeted near Gram's elbow.

"Don't do that." Gram slipped the plates into a

sink full of soap suds. "It'll just be a waste of time."

"Don't unpack?" Sam bit her lip. "Why not?"

Jake slid his chair away from the table with a screech. "You won't be staying long. That's why not."

Chapter Three ❧

SAM COULD HAVE SWORN the roast beef wiggled in her belly. What did Jake mean when he said she wasn't staying long?

"What Jake means," Gram said, "is we'll be leaving in the morning, so it makes no sense to unpack and repack." Gram watched Sam with gentle eyes. "I'll help you go through your clothes, though, and make sure you have what you'll need."

"Need for *what*?" Sam's shout surprised her as much as it did everyone else.

"Wyatt!" Gram tied her apron strings with a jerk. "Don't tell me you didn't explain."

"It was a surprise." Looking embarrassed, Dad turned to Sam. "We're moving the cattle from their winter pasture near the Calico Mountains up here to River Bend for the summer. It will take about a week and a half, because we do it the old-fashioned way, on horseback."

"It's easier on the calves," Jake added.

"Besides," Dad said, "it'll be a good way for you to get to know Ace and get back into the habit of riding."

"About *ten* hours a day!" Jake laughed.

Sam swallowed hard and returned his idiot grin, but she wasn't at all sure she was up to such riding. If only Jake hadn't said it like a dare.

Gram gave Sam a gentle push toward the door. "With all that riding ahead, you'd better get acquainted with your new horse."

Like Sam, Ace had good manners. Sam bridled Ace as Dad watched and the gelding accepted the bit as if it were candy-coated. He didn't puff up his belly when she saddled him, either, or move off while her left foot fumbled for the stirrup.

Sam and Ace circled the pasture with precision. Walk, jog, lope. The little bay made her look like an expert. All she had to do was stir her legs and the horse moved as she asked. And he was a *mustang*? Jake and Dad must be joking.

"You know what this is like?" Sam whispered, and the gelding's ears flicked back to listen. "Like you're just baby-sitting me, Ace."

Sam drew back on her reins and Ace stopped. He didn't shift from leg to leg, didn't pull against the bit. He did turn his head, noticing that Dad and Jake had walked away from the pasture fence. Bored stiff, probably.

Far off, Sam heard a neigh. Ace tossed his head and looked toward the foothills. Sam looked, too. She saw nothing, but Ace vibrated beneath her, nickering. Sam collected her reins an instant before Ace lunged from a standing stop into a full gallop.

Oh, no. Sam crashed back against the high Western cantle. Her teeth clacked together. She grabbed handfuls of Ace's coarse black mane and tried not to lose her stirrups.

The horse ran faster. Surely Ace wouldn't crash through the other horses clustered near the fence. Would he?

Sam leaned low against his extended neck and inched her hands down the reins, closer to the bit. As she remembered the last time she'd galloped this way, her pulse pounded in her neck. This time, she would *not* fall off.

Wind whipped Ace's mane into Sam's eyes. He was running away. Sam pulled the reins tighter, afraid she'd hurt his mouth. Ace ignored her. Then she tugged.

As if they'd run head-on into a brick wall, Ace stopped.

Sam slipped forward. The saddle horn poked her stomach, but that was all that kept her from sliding down his neck like a kid going headfirst down a playground slide. Thinking fast, she wrapped her arms around Ace's neck. Tight.

When Ace coughed, Sam made herself uncoil one arm. She really hoped no one was watching. Finally she took the other arm from around the gelding's neck.

Drawing a deep breath, she sat up, straightened her reins, and flexed her fingers. Her hands might be shaking from the pressure she'd applied to the bit, but she was pretty sure she was trembling because Ace had scared her half to death.

Could she ride this horse for ten days, with witnesses?

Beyond the pasture, near the barn, Jake waved. Sam pretended not to notice. No way was she going to take a hand off the reins to wave back.

Ace stamped one hoof and slung his head around to look at Sam. His big brown eyes glowed with intelligence and an equine sense of humor. For the first time, she noticed the white star high on his forehead.

"I apologize for thinking you were boring." Sam dismounted, keeping a grip on the reins. Her knees wobbled as she rubbed the gelding's warm neck. "You're a good boy, Ace."

The horse tossed his forelock to cover the star, then he followed obediently as Sam led.

Dismounting in the middle of the pasture might be silly. Leading Ace back to the barn, instead of riding him, might confirm Jake's opinion that she was a wimp. Still, there was no way in the world Sam would risk another one-horse stampede. Ace had proven he had the pride of a mustang.

A white quilt decorated with a patchwork star covered Sam's bed. The mattress was perfect—not too hard, not too soft. The pillow wasn't too puffy or too flat. Still, Sam couldn't sleep.

The full moon turned her bedroom wall into a movie screen. At least, that's what she'd thought as a child. Sam remembered staring at it, imagining stories in her own private theater.

In the best one, Blackie had worn the red and green Christmas ribbons she'd plaited into his mane. Together, he and Sam had rescued Mrs. Ott, her teacher, from stampeding buffalo. Sam had been too young to know that Nevada had no buffalo.

Sam stared at the wall, trying to recall the exact shape of Blackie's face. And then she knew why she couldn't. In the stories she'd told herself at night, she'd called the colt by his secret name.

A secret name, Jake had confided, was a code between human and horse. It would bind the colt to her, so that even in darkness, he'd know her. But horses heard many words, so the secret name had to sound like no other.

Zanzibar. Though the name was too fancy for a ranch horse, it had been their secret, and the colt had answered to it.

Down the hall, Dad and Gram slept. Outside Sam's window, the river sighed and coyotes called from the hills. They yipped, barked, then joined in a community howl.

Sam tried to enjoy the coyotes' wild song, but their nearness frightened her a little. One more thing she'd have to grow used to. Her bed sheets twisted around her legs. She kicked loose and rolled over on her stomach.

It wasn't late, but they'd leave for Red Rock, where Dad's cowboys were holding the cattle herd, by six A.M.

Sam reached for the wristwatch she'd left on her bedside table. Its numbers glowed in the dark. Ten o'clock. What would Aunt Sue be doing? Since it was summer, she'd have no papers to grade. She might be watching the news or reading. Maybe worrying about Sam.

Sam missed Aunt Sue for many reasons. The strongest was because she was Sam's mother's sister, and the closest Sam would ever come to knowing her mother, who'd died so young.

She'd been almost five when Mom died in a one-car accident. Skid marks showed she'd swerved to miss an animal, and her VW bug was upside down near an antelope migration area.

Sam remembered how Mom's auburn hair looked in braids with daisies stuck through the ends. She remembered her laughing and clapping in excitement.

And later, she remembered someone saying, "Louise just shoulda hit that critter," and someone answering, "Louise always had too big a heart."

Sam rolled back over and pulled the sheet over her face. She listened to her eyelashes tick back and forth.

She had a horse. She had Jake to remind her how to ride like a buckaroo. She had Dad. Why couldn't she be satisfied?

Sam threw back the covers, pulled on her pink robe, and crept down the hall. Quietly, she left the house.

As Sam closed the front door, the river shushed her. Crickets stopped chirping as if they were holding their breaths.

River Bend Ranch had no outside lights and she'd left the porch light off. Little by little, Sam's eyes grew used to the dark. A full moon turned the ranch grounds the black and white of an old photograph.

Sam stepped off the porch. Ahead, the sand and gravel driveway unrolled like a white velvet carpet leading to dark hills beyond the ranch gate. Night sky arched overhead with stars so bright, Sam picked out the Big Dipper instantly. A low nicker drew Sam's attention to the ten-acre pasture. It lay in a dark rectangle and horses moved across it in dreamy slowness.

And then a shower of gravel against rock made the horses jerk alert. One snorted. Another shied. They all looked toward the river.

Sam ran on tiptoe, wincing as pebbles jabbed her bare feet. The horses moved in a silent wave toward the far end of the pasture. Sam's toes jammed against a round rock and she almost stumbled. The horses broke into a trot and Sam ran faster, ignoring the stabbing stones.

The river rushed like wind as she neared it. When she saw him, Sam stopped.

Floating like a ghost, the stallion picked his way down the hillside on the other side of the river. His mane and tail rippled around him. His hooves were so soundless, he seemed to drift above the ground.

Would he jump the fence into the pasture? Would he clop across the wooden bridge or wade across the river?

The stallion reached the river and stopped.

Sam's pulse pounded. She couldn't believe this. The moonlight must be magical. She'd read myths of maidens who summoned unicorns, but Samantha Anne Forster was no fairy-tale princess.

The stallion didn't care. He splashed into the water, coming to her.

His hooves grated on river rock. Halfway across, he stood still, knee-deep in his own reflection. This close, Sam could see the stallion wasn't white. His hide was dappled gray and silver, like the surface of the moon. He was the same stallion who'd rescued the herd this morning.

Sam didn't move. She barely breathed.

The stallion's nostrils flared, drawing in her scent. For a moment, he lifted his head, testing the breeze, and then his eyes returned to her.

Sam's heart thudded so hard she feared the stallion heard. Only one horse had ever studied her with such friendship.

If this was a dream, Sam never wanted to wake.

The stallion arched his neck and pawed three times.

Water drops scattered like diamonds.

What did he want? He was a mustang, a wild thing. If she whispered or held out her hand, he'd run. Then it struck her. What if he was hers? What if he was Smoke's son, a black colt turned white?

Sam had no chance to find out. As if he'd read her mind, the stallion flung his head high. Water churned as he wheeled on his hind legs and launched onto the bank in a single leap.

Mist hung where he had been. The river flowed smooth again and the crickets chirped.

No one could know the stallion had stood there.

Except for Sam. She knew the truth. The truth was, her dream had come true.

By moonlight, Zanzibar had returned to her, at last.

Chapter Four ❧

GRAM PULLED THE PILLOW off Sam's head and kissed her cheek. "Good morning," she said.

Sam wasn't so sure. When she gazed out her bedroom window, it still looked like night.

Minutes later, Sam sat beside Gram in the white van, which served as a modern chuck wagon. Sam focused on the red taillights bobbing on the road ahead. Jake and Dad drove the truck and pulled a horse trailer big enough to carry Ace, Dad's horse, Banjo, and Jake's black mare, Witch.

Sam stayed awake long enough to drink the cocoa Gram had insisted she bring. As soon as her eyelids closed, though, she imagined a silver stallion. Wild as the wind, he'd returned to River Bend on the same night she had. *He was Zanzibar,* she thought drowsily, *and he was real.*

Sam slept through much of the drive to Red Rock, where Dad's three cowboys had joined Linc

Slocum's men to gather range cattle from both ranches into a single large herd.

When Sam awoke, they'd arrived and Gram was hustling her out of the van.

Hundreds of cattle, mothers and calves with fuzzy red-brown fur and white faces, were mooing and bawling, worried by the two trucks and the men on horseback.

Sam climbed out, feeling a little shy. She shouldn't. Many of these cattle belonged to her family, but she'd been too young to go on drives before. Now her time in the city made her feel like an outsider.

Then Gram stood beside her, indicating which cowboys rode for Dad.

"Dallas has been on the River Bend for years," Gram said. "You probably remember him."

Sam did, and she smiled. The gray-haired man was the only cowboy on foot. He stood talking to Dad. Sam thought his bowed legs looked better suited to gripping a horse than walking.

"And that's Ross." Gram nodded to a man sitting tall in the saddle of a Quarter horse. "That man is so quiet, he hardly talks to anyone, even your father."

Pepper was the youngest cowboy, nicknamed for his chili pepper red hair. He glanced at Sam, then looked away.

"How old is he?" Sam asked. "He looks like a kid."

"A year older than Jake," Gram said with a sigh.

"That boy ran away from his home in Idaho. Far north in Idaho, near the Canadian border. Said it was too cold." Gram smiled and lowered her voice. "He has no idea your father tracked down his parents to tell them he was okay."

As Sam pulled on her favorite black sweater, she felt a surge of pride in her father. She ran the names through her mind once more. Dallas. Ross. Pepper.

They'd all eat dinner together tonight and she'd have to start learning the other cowboys' names, too.

Gram would cook for all of them. Each day, she'd drive the van to the place where the crew would camp for the night. She'd arrive hours before the slow-moving cattle.

Gram would get the gear down from the carrier atop the van and she'd pitch the tents. Next, she'd build a campfire. She'd roast meat over the fire, but she'd cook the rest of the meal on a stove in the back of the chuck wagon. By the time the herd arrived, the cowboys would just have time to clean up for dinner.

Gram's job sounded like a lot of work. Riding Ace all day and watching the cattle trot back toward their summer pastures at River Bend sounded like a vacation.

"Hey, princess." Jake's joking voice made Sam turn. "Think you can give me a hand with these horses?"

The cowboys were watching. Sam could feel them

wondering how Wyatt Forster's city slicker daughter would do.

What if Ace tossed his head too high for her to reach? Or refused the bit? If he planted a hoof on the toe of her new boot and wouldn't move, could she keep from yelping?

The River Bend cowboys might not mock her, but Linc Slocum's men could be a different story.

Sam shot a quick glance their way. She probably just imagined their sneers.

Jake had unloaded all three horses and tied their lead ropes to rings on the trailer. Now he carried a saddle on each arm, as if they didn't weigh an ounce. As Sam moved in next to him, Ace swung his head around as far as the rope allowed. His warm breath clouded the cold morning air. He nuzzled her arm.

Surprised and pleased, Sam rubbed the gelding's brown neck. He knew her.

"Good boy," she said, then turned to Jake. "Where's Ace's bridle?"

Sam reached up to lift the halter off the bay's head.

"Put that back on," Jake ordered as he handed her Ace's bridle. "Put this on over the halter and get a bit in his mouth before you untie him." Jake shook his head. "You don't want him hightailing it out of here before you can say good-bye."

"I don't need lessons," Sam muttered.

She did it Jake's way, even though Ace was so well behaved, she didn't need to.

With the feel of eyes watching each move, Sam smoothed on Ace's saddle blanket. Bracing her arm muscles, she grabbed the saddle and swung it into place on Ace's back.

As she tightened the cinch, she felt smug.

As she tucked her boot in the stirrup, she was confident.

But when she placed all her weight on that stirrup and started to vault up into the saddle, it slipped sideways. Sam wished she could turn invisible.

The cowboys laughed.

Though she jerked her boot free of the stirrup and hopped back quick enough to keep from falling, she must've looked real funny.

"Happens all the time, honey." Dad was beside her right away.

"I know," Sam said. She didn't want sympathy.

"Oldest trick that pony has," Dallas added.

"I know that," Sam repeated. And she did.

Yesterday, she'd checked Ace's belly to see if he'd puffed up so the cinch would hang loose when he released his breath. Today, she'd trusted him.

She bent to lift the saddle. When she heard movement, she looked over her shoulder to see Jake step forward, as if to help.

"Don't even think about it," she muttered.

Jake held his hands up as if holding off an attack,

and stepped back again.

Sam didn't need a mirror to know she was blushing.

Once she put the saddle right, she tapped Ace's belly to make him exhale, then pulled the cinch snug. Ace stamped one hoof and swung his head around to give her a glare.

She looked him right in the eyes.

"Look insulted all you want," she whispered. "But if you won't trust me, I can't trust you."

Ace's black-tipped ears flicked back and forth, waiting for another word. But Sam was done talking.

Once in the saddle, she consulted her watch, just to avoid the cowboys' amused eyes. It was only seven o'clock in the morning.

Because her face was still so tight and hot it hurt, riding out on her first cattle drive wasn't as much fun as she'd expected.

Gram waved and the cows and calves increased their calls to a moo racket she never could have imagined. All the animals wore Slocum's double-S brand, or the backward *F* for Forster. The herd strung out across the range, until they stretched about a quarter mile in front of Sam and Ace. The riders moved into a rough formation around the herd.

Dad rode in front on Banjo. A few cowboys rode on each side. Sam, half hidden in dust, brought up the rear.

A few times, she tried to ride closer to the other riders, but Linc Slocum's big palomino struck out with a hoof, trying to kick Ace.

"Sorry, little lady," Slocum said, with his tooth-paste-commercial grin.

Slocum wore snakeskin boots, brass-rowelled spurs, and a long, brown duster more appropriate for Hollywood than rural Nevada.

His too-friendly attitude might have bothered her more, except that other riders were unwilling to talk. And when she rode too close to Jake, Witch whirled with her mouth open, looking as if she'd peel Ace's nose with her bared teeth.

Sam reined Ace in, urging him away from danger. He thanked her by giving a buck. Sam's teeth clacked together. Before she remembered not to, she grabbed the saddle horn for balance. By the time Ace quit pulling against the bit, dancing as if he wanted to run for home, they were bringing up the rear, again.

So this was her dream come true. Samantha Forster, the boss's daughter, blinked against the dust raised by hundreds of hooves. She stayed there all morning as the herd headed west, toward the Calico Mountains.

Sam had just looked up at the sun, directly over-head, when Jake appeared, making Witch walk beside Ace, whether or not she wanted to.

"We're not stopping for lunch," Jake said. "I have some jerky in my saddlebags, though, if you're hungry."

"I'm fine," Sam said, even though she had nothing

but the water in her canteen, and it tasted metallic and warm.

She didn't care about lunch. She only cared about riding well enough to return to the range in search of the Phantom. So far, she wasn't doing so well.

Since it was getting hot, Sam wiggled out of her black sweater and tied it around her waist. She settled her old brown felt cowboy hat with one hand. It still fit after two years. She peered out from its shade.

Sam tried to read Jake's expression, but his lean jaw stayed in its usual set position and he looked straight ahead. Would he mention her terrible morning and say she had a long way to go before she was the rider she used to be?

Sam wouldn't give him a chance.

"How old are these calves?" she blurted, pointing at the leggy babies, walking beside their mothers. Most weren't as tall as a Labrador retriever.

"A couple months old," Jake said. "We wait 'til they've all been dropped before we move them."

To Sam, *dropped* seemed a strange word for being born, especially because cows were such gentle mothers.

Now, for instance, she saw a cow stop and use her huge pink tongue to wash her calf's face. The herd flowed around her on both sides, but she cleaned her baby as the other cattle passed her by.

As soon as the cow and calf stood alone, Ace bolted forward, as if to chase her, and Sam drew the reins tight.

"You need to keep loose reins on a cow horse. Remember?" Jake said. He still didn't look at her, and he said it so quietly, no one else could have heard.

"Every time I loosen up, he goes his own way," she admitted.

When Jake said nothing, she decided he was only trying to help. She bit the inside of her cheek and loosened the reins.

Ace bolted into a jouncing trot.

"Relax. You're not riding in a horse show. Don't grab that horn again, Samantha. What are you thinking?"

She was thinking that her new horse hated her.

Ace veered away from the herd and lengthened his stride. Sam jerked the reins tight again.

She didn't speak when Jake stopped his horse, too. She couldn't risk sounding weepy.

Jake bumped his black hat away from his serious brown eyes.

Mustang eyes. When they were kids, Jake had told her Shoshone tales. One story described the old times when humans were animals. Ten-year-old Jake, with his glossy black hair and lively leaps, just knew he'd been a mustang in the old times. He'd been equally convinced Sam was once a mosquito—a buzzing, troublesome pest.

Now, Jake looked at her with frustration, as if he might still believe it.

"What?" she demanded. After a single day on the ranch, she was sick of trying to prove herself.

"Nothing."

"It's not *nothing*. Didn't you outgrow that?"

He shrugged with a teasing grin, as if he remembered their kid days, too. Half of Sam wanted to go back to being playmates. Half of her wanted to confide in Jake. He was older, and a wizard with horses. He'd know what to do about the silver stallion.

But she'd waited too long. Jake tugged his hat back over his eyes. All business, he nodded toward her horse.

"Ace is testing you, is all," Jake said. "Hang in there."

He rode on ahead.

Any curl that had ever been in Sam's hair was gone. The short wisps hung into her eyes. She needed lip balm for the dry skin on her mouth and her cheeks felt chalky with desert dirt.

At first, she thought the white triangles ahead looked like teeth poking up out of the sand and sagebrush. She squinted and blinked. Finally, she recognized the tents and Gram's chuck wagon. Then she caught the aroma of baking biscuits.

This time when Sam loosened her reins, Ace read her mind. He trotted past the cattle, past the cowboys, past Dad, whom she hadn't seen since morning.

With a rolling hand motion, Dad was instructing the cowboys to urge the cattle into the tight herd they'd been in this morning.

Rejuvenated by the smells ahead, Sam winked at Dad and pointed at the herd.

"I'm going to leave this to you professionals," she said. As she moved off, Dad gave a short laugh.

Longing for a cold soda, Sam let Ace swing into a lope, and settled back into the saddle. This time, the signal made him stop short in a haze of dust.

"Careful of my campfire," Gram scolded, but she didn't sound cranky. She looked neat, with a white apron over her jeans, as she pointed toward an enclosure made of portable plastic fence. "Follow Pepper," she added.

The young red-haired cowboy had dismounted. He unsaddled his dun gelding next to the corral and left his reins trailing on the dirt. *Ground-tying*, it was called. Cowboys trained their mounts to stay around, without being tied, but Sam didn't think it would work with Ace.

Before she could give it a try, Jake appeared to stand at Ace's head.

"Thanks," Sam said, but she got the distinct feeling that Jake was baby-sitting her. She'd swung one leg toward the ground when she heard him mumble something that sounded like, "*Long ride*," but she wasn't sure enough to answer.

He added something she did hear.

"Your knees are apt to be a bit wobbly."

"I'm fine," Sam insisted.

The warning irritated her, mostly because it was true. She'd been in the saddle for nine hours and Jake knew she wasn't used to it. As her boots touched the ground, her legs felt liquid and unsteady. She hated to use Ace for balance, but it was better than falling over backward.

The chores of checking Ace's feet, of unsaddling, and juggling that floppy gate before she turned him out, loomed like the task of climbing a mountain.

"I'll take him," Jake offered.

"Fat chance," Sam said. As she lifted her chin to look up at him, her hat slipped off her hair. She caught it and slammed it back on her head.

"If there's one thing I know, it's to take care of my horse before I pamper myself," she said. "It doesn't matter how much I want to pry off these boots or wash my face. Ace comes first."

For a minute, she thought Jake would give her a pat on the back. He didn't, but the satisfied look on his face was enough.

As Sam squatted to lift Ace's hooves and check them for stones, she felt so pleased, she forgot to worry about all the other cowboys she'd have to face at dinner.

Chapter Five ❧

𝒯HE JOSHING STARTED after dinner, as Sam swallowed a last bite of peach cobbler. Dad stood with one boot on a tree stump, staring into the fire. Jake stood a few steps away, leaning against the chuck wagon. Sam sat perched on a rock between them.

She looked past the men eating around the campfire, off into the desert painted lavender by the setting sun. The herd was still restless, but a few mounted cowboys circled them, turning back cows trying to make a break for the familiar territory they'd left behind. The cattle wouldn't be left unattended for a minute, until they reached home pastures at River Bend and Slocum's ranch.

Sam wanted to do her part, but she felt tired down to her toenails. She hoped Dallas wouldn't tell her to "nighthawk." If she rode four more hours tonight, she'd be facedown in her mashed potatoes by this time tomorrow night.

One of Linc Slocum's cowboys set his plate aside and looked her way. Named Flick, the man was renowned for his roping skill and his long, drooping mustache.

"That pony was doing his best to keep the herd together," Flick said.

Sam couldn't pretend he wasn't talking to her. Everyone knew he was. And his comment awakened her to the reason Ace had kept bolting.

A cow pony was like a sheepdog. Ace's job was to keep the herd together. When that cow had stopped to lick her calf, Ace had thought she was lagging. Sam had been so set on controlling Ace, she'd stopped him from doing his job.

Apologies streamed across her mind, but she didn't utter them. This was a test. The cowboys were waiting to see if the city girl would act offended or burst into tears.

Neither.

Suddenly, Sam knew what to do. A cowboy wouldn't make a fuss explaining.

"Yep," she said, nodding. "He was."

Had she heard her father chuckle?

"Sam's been gone awhile, but she's on the comeback trail," Dallas said as he whittled a stick.

Sam would bet everyone was remembering the accident.

Linc Slocum confirmed it. "Can't wipe out that mustang blood in one generation," he said. "I heard the horse that throwed you was a mustang."

"Half," Sam said, though she hated to give Slocum an instant of satisfaction.

"Range rats," muttered Flick.

Sam couldn't resist answering that, too.

"You know *musteño,* the Spanish word 'mustang' comes from, just means strays," Sam pointed out. "So some will be good horses, and some ordinary."

"Smoke, her colt's sire, was the best working horse I ever had," Dad said. "He was a mustang. Same color as an iron skillet and just as tough. Smoke could stay out all day and be fresh at night. He was kinda wise, from looking out for himself on the range."

"Seems to me there's a mustang you've been trying to put a rope on, Linc," Jake said.

Slocum stood up, as if he'd been insulted. He made a big show of lighting a cigarette and threw his match on the ground.

Jake poured more coffee from the pot suspended over the campfire.

When Slocum figured out Jake wasn't worried that he'd offended him, Slocum gave a short laugh.

"That Phantom's the only one out there worth anything," Slocum said.

Sam shivered. When she'd met Slocum, he'd known a surprising amount about Blackie. Could he suspect her lost colt had grown up to be the silver stallion?

"Those broomtails eat like vacuum cleaners," Slocum complained. "I wish they'd take 'em all off the range and keep it for cattle."

"Your herd looks fine, Linc." Dallas stood and stretched. He started giving orders. "It's eight o'clock. Time for me, Jake, and two of your boys to give those riders a break." Dallas gestured toward the herd. "If the night riders get sleepy, your fat, sassy heifers might lope out of here.

"Rest of you, turn in. Nighthawk shifts change at midnight and four."

Slocum tried to finish his argument over the sound of men putting tin dishes in the dishpan.

"It's pure luck it's been a wet year," Slocum shouted. "With plenty of graze . . ."

When his voice trailed off, Sam thought no one noticed.

She was wrong. Later, Sam went to find Gram and found her tidying up. Gram looked glad for the company, but she tsked her tongue and nodded toward Slocum.

"This time last year, the closest he'd been to a cow was a T-bone steak."

Sam laughed, and admired Gram's skill. She'd already set the chuck wagon back in order. Potatoes and onions sat in mesh bags next to a burlap sack of rice. Cans of fruit, beans, and coffee shared space with soap and first aid supplies. But there was much left to do.

"Can I help you wash dishes?" Sam offered.

"I don't mind doing them. My hands are a little stiff from driving. Warm water will feel good." Gram smoothed her hand over Sam's chopped-off hair. "You'll have plenty to keep you busy this week without doing my chores, too. Might as well crawl into your sleeping bag now. I'll try not to wake you when I come to bed."

As Sam moved away from the campfire, it got darker. Still, she knew Jake was following her before she made it to the tent she'd share with Gram.

Sam didn't remember noticing Jake wore spurs, but they rang in the darkness as he took long strides to catch up with her.

"What'd you do with your gear?" he asked.

"My—?"

"Saddle, bridle, saddle blanket?" Jake gave her ten seconds to think. "You left them on the ground, Sam. You're in charge of your own tack, so go pick it up, clean it off, and put it where you can find it." Jake gave her shoulder a shake and Sam wondered how he could still have so much energy. "Nothing says 'tenderfoot' like being the last one saddled up in the morning."

Though she yearned for the warm cocoon of her sleeping bag, Sam borrowed a flashlight from Gram and found the spot near the corral, where she'd dropped her gear.

Crickets chirped as she shook out her saddle

blanket, turned her stirrups, and cleaned her bit. Suddenly, every horse in the makeshift corral threw a drowsy head up, ears pricked to attention toward the dark shape of the Calico Mountains.

Sam listened. The crickets had hushed, so she heard the movement of cattle, but nothing more.

It couldn't be Zanzibar. Gram had said they'd driven seventy-eight miles this morning, and traveling cross-country, they'd drive the cattle fifty miles back to the ranch. A horse couldn't cover that much territory in a day. One who could, had to be a ghost.

Sam's knees creaked as she stood, slowly and silently.

"Sam?" Dad's voice came through the darkness.

So much for quiet. Oh well, the horses had probably only heard a coyote or deer.

"Over here." Sam picked up her gear, determined to take it into her tent for the night.

"How're you doing, hon?" Dad's voice told Sam he'd worried over her, but he hadn't let the other cowboys know.

"I'm fine," Sam settled under Dad's arm as he took her saddle in one arm and hugged her against his side with the other.

"I wanted to give you time to get used to being home, but your grandmother said 'no.' She said this would show our neighbors you were home for good, and that I, well, trusted you."

Dad stopped walking for a minute, and Sam

wished she could see his face.

"Every calf will be worth his weight in dollars come market time. The sooner we get them home, the less chance harm can come to them."

When she'd been eleven, Dad had never mentioned money. Or maybe money hadn't seemed important to her. Now, Sam heard the worry in his voice.

"I won't do anything to slow you down, Dad."

"You're doing fine, Sam. It's just—" Dad cleared his throat. "Every small rancher in Nevada feels the land vultures circling, looking to buy failed ranches. We can't afford any mistakes."

"No more tenderfoot mistakes," she promised. "I'll watch you and Jake and the other hands and do what they do. I promise. You can assign me to nighthawk, even."

"Dallas is the trail boss. He decides who does what."

"Why? If you're the owner, shouldn't you be in charge?"

"We're doing this drive with Slocum," Dad's voice turned hard. "In case of conflict, if the two of us claim an unbranded cow, for instance, we need a man in charge who doesn't stand to profit."

Dad stood with her outside the little white tent and waited for her to understand.

"I get it," she said, but a yawn clouded her words and Dad chuckled.

"Enough heavy talk. Hop in bed, sleepyhead. Dawn comes mighty early on the range."

Next morning, Sam woke to the sound of lowing cattle.

She pulled jeans past aching muscles, yanked boots over her warm socks, and managed to devour a stack of hotcakes with maple syrup before she and Ace put on a rodeo.

Mindful of Jake's warning, Sam was first to catch her horse and saddle him. Even in the crowded corral, in half-light, Ace was easy to find. He cowered in the far corner, facing the other horses.

Soon, she found out why. She smoothed the saddle blanket on his back and gave his flank a pat. Her hand came back, sticky with blood.

"Oh, Ace, poor baby." She pressed her cheek against the gelding's neck as she remembered Witch lunging at Ace with bared teeth.

In spite of the bites, Ace still had the spirit to try puffing his stomach against the cinch. When that trick didn't work, he kept his teeth closed, refusing the bit.

"You're like a little kid who refuses his vegetables," Sam whispered as she slipped her thumb into the corner of Ace's lips to lever open his jaws.

Once Sam mounted, Ace settled down. Since the other cowboys were just finishing breakfast, she considered what to do.

What if she rode up to the chuck wagon and asked Gram for a cup of coffee? She didn't really like coffee, but it might look cool to sit there on Ace, with one of those blue-speckled mugs.

That was how Sam came to be right near the chuck wagon, where everyone could watch, when Ace bowed his head between his front hooves, kicked out his hind legs, and began to buck.

As her chin flew forward to strike her breastbone, Sam's hat flew off. It cartwheeled right under Ace's nose. He reared as if it were a demon and Sam's head snapped back. Then he did it all over again. Sam heard voices as if someone were switching between stations on a radio.

"Sam—

"Ride 'em—

"—away from the—"

"Holy Hannah, hang on!"

The loudest voice was the one in her head. *No more tenderfoot mistakes.* She must stick to Ace no matter what.

As Ace began running, Sam tightened her reins. But when she saw he meant to jump the campfire, she gave him his head.

Up, stretch, over.

In a flurry of hooves, he headed for the tents. Before he reached them, Ace bucked some more. Brown hide, gray dirt, blue sky, she caught swinging views of the world before memory told her what to do.

Sam leaned back, grabbed the right rein, and pulled it toward her hip. Ace couldn't help turning in a circle. He didn't like being dizzy, and finally stopped. For a minute, his legs stayed braced apart. His sides heaved with effort. Then, he shook like a wet dog, swished his tail, and waited, ears up, for directions.

For a minute, Sam wondered what to do. *Jake.* As temporary wrangler, he'd be over by the corral. Maybe he could explain why Ace had chosen this morning to go insane.

Dallas gave an approving nod as Sam and Ace passed. Another cowboy winked. Pepper handed Sam her hat. She must have done all right. At least that's what Sam thought until she saw Jake.

"Jake?"

Down on one knee, he didn't look up from checking a horse's pastern, even though he must have heard her voice.

"Hey Jake," she said again, aware she sounded breathless.

"Don't talk to me, Samantha."

Sam froze in surprise. Even though she hadn't fallen off, she'd committed some awful tenderfoot sin.

"Why are you mad?" Sam felt a clutch of guilt. "Was it— Did I pull on his mouth too hard?"

"No. Nothing like that."

"If you think I was mean to him—" Sam pictured the scene all over again. "Honest, I couldn't think what else to do."

Jake wouldn't face her. Staring at the back of his head told her nothing.

When Jake looked sideways, she followed his glance. At a distance, she saw Dad, tight-lipped and white-faced. They were both mad, though she'd hoped to make them proud.

Confused, Sam rode over to Dallas. As the trail boss, he handed out work assignments. Maybe he'd explain where she'd gone wrong.

Sam only had time for a sigh, before Dallas began talking.

"You did fine," Dallas said. "Don't pay Jake and Wyatt any mind. You scared 'em, that's all."

Sam didn't think that made sense, but Dallas hadn't asked for her opinion.

"You and Ace came to a fork in the road," he said. "And you took charge."

"Thanks, I—"

"That's that. Now, you ride drag again. You've got a bandanna. Today, wear it. And if Ace wants to cut off strays, you let him.

"You know how to ride, Sam, but that fall's made you skittish. Just keep your reins low and loose in your left hand, and let the palm of your right hand rest on your thigh. Sway with him and he'll do the rest. You're not going to fall."

Sam took Dallas's advice to heart and the second day of the drive was better than the first. It was a breezy day, but hot enough to roll up the cuffs of her pale blue shirt.

She and Ace had reached an agreement. Sam went along for the ride as he dropped into a low, stalking-cat posture to turn back cows. In return, he followed her directions on everything else.

The compromise turned yesterday's stiff trot into a smooth jog. Relaxed, Sam wondered if Dallas was right about that other thing. Had her wild ride scared Dad and Jake because they still worried over her accident?

"Well, they'd better get over it," Sam told Ace.

At noon, Dallas directed her to change horses. She'd need Ace fresh tonight, he explained, for nighthawking.

"You're a sight better rider than Slocum and he's next in the rotation after you." Dallas glanced toward Slocum where he sat, smoking, on a red dun horse.

The sun's angle turned Slocum's belt buckle to dazzling silver and Dallas made a sound of disgust.

"I'd bet my next three paychecks he bought that trophy buckle in a pawnshop," Dallas said, then looked Sam straight in the eye. "Sam, some things can't be bought. You were born to ride, so get out there and do it."

Sam felt such a zing of surprise, she had to concentrate as Dallas went on.

"Jake'll wake you at midnight when he goes off shift," Dallas said. "Get to bed early and rest up."

Sam changed her gear to a roan mare named Strawberry and wondered if Ace would enjoy the break. Turned in with the group of spare horses, the remuda, he'd still walk along, trailing the herd, but no rider would tell him what to do.

Pulling her cinch snug, Sam thought about tonight. When Jake came to wake her, she'd make the most of the quiet time while the rest of the camp slept. She'd find out what had made him mad, even if she had to tickle it out of him, as she had in the old days.

Sam's heart lifted at that idea, then skyrocketed as she thought of something even better.

Oh, wow. For four hours, she and another cowboy would ride in opposite directions around the herd. They would pass each other only once in a while. If the feeling she'd had last night was real, the Phantom had followed her to the desert. Maybe he'd spot her, riding alone.

It was improbable, but not impossible. Dad had told her mustangs had hideaways and trails that no people knew.

The thought gave Sam chills. As soon as the first star of evening glowed in the sky, she'd wish her lost colt would come to her again.

Chapter Six ☙

SAM TURNED UP the collar of her fleece-lined jacket. She couldn't find her favorite black sweater, or she would have worn it, too. Saddle leather chilled her knees even through her jeans. It might be summer, but nights in the high Nevada desert were cold.

Ninety percent of your body heat escapes from your head, or so Dad had told her years ago. Sam tugged her Stetson down tighter and Ace side-stepped.

"Settle down, boy." Sam adjusted her hat on its new string.

The leather strips, smoothly braided by Pepper, were knotted a couple of inches below her chin.

"Stampede strings," Pepper had called them as he helped her attach them after dinner. "So you don't lose your hat next time."

Smiling, Sam patted Ace's neck. Her watch said it

was after three. Ace should be tired. She couldn't imagine why he kept arching his neck, or why his barrel vibrated with a low nicker.

Then she saw the Phantom.

The desert floor stretched around him, level and smooth as a marble dance floor. The stallion snorted plumes of breath into the night. Starlight caught the dust, which drifted from each hoof to create a shimmering trail behind him.

Sam held her breath, joining in the silence. He was the most beautiful thing she'd ever seen, a silver dragon horse, spun of moonbeams and magic.

Suddenly, the stallion's low neigh shattered the quiet. He reared, shaking wild torrents of mane, then launched himself toward them, at a run.

He wasn't going to stop. From afar, he'd looked fine-boned, but as the stallion thundered closer, Sam saw Phantom had the broad, powerful chest of a mature stallion. He galloped straight for Ace, ready to ram.

"Go!" Sam leaned low on Ace's neck. She clapped her heels against his sides, asking, then *telling* him to run.

Even when she smacked his hindquarters with her palm, Ace only moved a few stiff-legged steps. Hopeless, Sam tried to discourage the stallion.

"Stop!" she shouted.

The stallion faltered a step, struck Ace a glancing blow, then turned to lay his muscled neck over Ace's back.

The horses stood together and the stallion's head was so close, Sam could have touched him—but she didn't. She was a little afraid. This must be some sort of dominance move, because Ace didn't fight.

The stallion was big. And this close, Sam couldn't deny he was real. He smelled like an animal who'd run long and hard. Though his hide glowed silver with an overlay of dapples delicate as gray lace, much of his fur was rough with dried sweat.

The horses drew apart. Together, they tossed their muzzles skyward. It must have been a signal of agreement, because suddenly, they were running.

With a peculiar rocking movement, the two horses ran side by side. Sam had ridden galloping horses before, but this was a faster gait, unnamed by man. Ace flung his legs out to their limits, and the stallion matched each movement.

I'm being kidnapped, Sam thought. It would be foolhardy to jump, but she couldn't catch a breath.

Night wind roared into her face, sealing off her nose and lips, ripping the hat from her head and flinging it to the end of the stampede string, where it flew like a kite.

Ace ignored the gentle pressure on the reins. Sam increased the pull and settled hard in the saddle. Nothing worked. Ace was running away.

Sam's feelings between fear and enchantment battled within her. She didn't dare fall. At this pace, she'd break an arm, leg, or ribs for sure. The sharp and heavy hooves might miss her, but her head would crash against the desert floor. Again.

And yet, Sam couldn't suppress her excitement.

Eight hooves pounded like a tribal drumbeat. Night wind sang past her ears and pulled her hair. The scents of sagebrush and horse flooded her senses. This was the wildest adventure of her life. She only hoped she lived long enough to brag to Jake.

When the stallion put on a burst of speed and cut across their path, Ace followed. The ground beneath grew steeper and rockier. The Phantom swerved onto a secret trail.

If they turned back now, could Ace find his way to the herd? They'd galloped at least three miles, maybe five. Could she return alone, if Ace dumped her and traded his bridled days for life as a mustang?

As the stallion crowded in front, his hooves rang on smooth rock. If she could see her surroundings, Sam thought she'd wheel Ace and force him back toward the herd. But she couldn't see. They might be on the edge of a meadow or a cliff.

The darkness broke. Moonlight glowed on the stallion's muscled haunches, but just for an instant. The trail had become a tunnel. Stone grazed Sam's knuckles as Ace pressed against the rock wall on the right.

In a shaft of light, Sam saw the stallion's pale head lower. Ace ducked, too.

Just in time, Sam imitated them before a cold

stone ceiling scrubbed her shirt back and grated over the bumps of her spine.

Ace moved slowly, carefully, but the Phantom bolted ahead. The sounds greeting him told Sam exactly where they were, though she'd been here only in her dreams.

One neigh was followed by another, and another. A foal squealed and horses rustled through grass. The stone ceiling ended. When Sam stared up, she felt dizzy. It looked as if a huge bowl full of stars had been clapped over the top of this mustang hideaway.

She had only seconds to marvel, before Ace bucked.

"Steady," Sam said, but she gave up without a fight.

As Ace came to a nervous stop, Sam knotted her reins together. Then she scrambled down, kicking free of her stirrups before he bolted away.

Dark horse shadows rippled against the moonlit cliffs, looking huge, then merging with the night. Sam knew it was too dark to try to leave. She didn't want to, anyway.

Sam worried about getting back to camp. She worried the cowboys would come searching, find her and call her worse than a tenderfoot. But Sam believed few humans would ever experience a night like this, and she wouldn't give it up.

As she settled against a boulder, hoofbeats told Sam that the Phantom was circling his herd, checking.

She heard a foal nursing and the quiet rushing of a stream.

Sam snuggled deeper into her coat. She felt surprisingly warm and satisfied. Ace was home. It was only fair she give him a chance to enjoy it.

Faint sunlight shone through Sam's closed eyelids, but she didn't open them. As soon as she did, the dreamy valley of wild horses would probably vanish. She'd be back in the tent she shared with Gram. Maybe even back in Aunt Sue's San Francisco apartment.

Then Ace whuffled his lips across her hand and Sam opened her eyes. She took a deep breath, let it out, and for the first time, she understood what it meant to "feast your eyes."

She couldn't count all the mustangs, but she tried to memorize them. Bays and blacks, red sorrels and honey chestnuts grazed beside buckskins, duns, and grays. More lean and muscular than even hardworking ranch horses, they looked wild, but their coats gleamed with health.

As if he felt her watching, the Phantom strode forward, standing between Sam and his mares and foals.

Protective and wary, the stallion squared off, ready to fight for his family.

Sam knew she should leave. Dad and Jake were

probably looking for her and they could find this haven. Worse, Linc Slocum could find it — Dallas had told her that Slocum had the nighthawk shift after hers.

Sam stood and the mares scattered. Reins trailing, Ace moved along behind her, willing to carry her home. But Sam had to try one thing before she mounted up.

She walked toward the stallion.

"Zanzibar," she whispered.

His neck arched until his chin bumped his chest, but his eyes stayed fixed on Sam. His ears strained so far forward, they nearly touched at the points. His skin shivered as if he felt the same goose bumps she did.

"Zanzibar, remember me?"

The stallion tilted his head, listening. A clump of silver mane fell aside, exposing a scar on his neck.

Pitying him for whatever accident had caused the scar, Sam held out her hand.

"Poor boy," she murmured, but her move was a mistake.

Too much, too soon.

The stallion backed away. As his band scattered, Sam noticed a buckskin with a black dorsal stripe and a dun mare and foal, with dark slanted stripes on their legs.

They could be throwbacks to ancient horses. Prehistoric horses had such markings, but Sam didn't know horses lived in this valley. Sam felt a surge of affection mixed with loyalty. She'd come here by accident, but now it was her duty to protect these animals and their home.

She must leave without startling them into a stampede. Ace stood nearby, apparently willing to go, but she'd misread his equine mind before. If he put up a fuss, the herd might run from the valley—right into Slocum.

Sam decided to lead Ace instead of mounting.

"Ace?" She patted her leg to get his attention. The gelding stepped forward.

His willingness tugged at Sam's heart. Ace still had welts from the bites in the camp corral. He couldn't want to return. Yet here, too, Ace was an outsider.

Sam caught the reins and vowed to talk with Jake about horse behavior. She'd help Ace if she could.

Sam moved as if she wore ankle weights. She had to go, but longed to stay. She stepped carefully and kept her eyes fixed on the passage ahead. That tunnel would lead her out of the valley. Ace lagged at the end of his reins as she led him.

Ace stopped, and Sam heard the thudding of other hooves. She looked back in time to see the Phantom touch noses with the gelding.

Entering the passage was easy, but the rock tunnel closed around her, dark and creepy. Sam blinked, wondering how Ace walked without hesitation.

She could see nothing. It smelled damp, like a cave. She imagined bats sleeping just overhead and her boots slipped on the smooth stone underfoot.

By the time Sam and Ace emerged from the tunnel, daybreak had turned the sky peachy-pink. The high desert lay silent and calm, but Sam wasn't sure what to do.

They stood atop a hill. Not a huge hill—it was about the size of three houses piled one on top of another—but it was steep and she could see no way through the sharp-edged shale covering it all the way down to level ground.

There must be a way down. In last night's darkness, the horses had jogged up with so little hesitation, they might have been traveling on a bridle path.

Sam decided to trust Ace. She swung into the saddle, gave the horse his head, and prayed he wouldn't fall.

As Ace started down, Sam stared between his ears and swayed in the saddle, trying to ride loose. Even when Ace's hoof made something skid away, starting an avalanche that sounded like a crash of dropped dishes, she didn't tell Ace what to do.

Dad had taught her horses were prey animals: Their brains believed that something fast and hungry was always lurking nearby. If a horse shied at a blowing branch, it was because a crouching cougar might have caused that movement. If a horse refused to cross a creek, it was because his legs moved slowly in water and something on the bank might notice and come after him.

Horses knew pursuit could happen anytime. Speed was their secret weapon. They fought to stay on all four fleet feet. So Sam trusted Ace to pick his way down the hillside, safely.

Just the same, Sam didn't notice the approaching rider until she had reached level ground.

"Samantha!" Linc Slocum's bellow surprised two sage hens into flight.

Sam ran a hand over her short hair. Its tousled appearance was a dead giveaway that she hadn't just gone out for an early ride. Sleeping against a rock had left her hair mashed in some places, sticking out in wild swoops in others.

Sam hoped her hat would cover the worst of it.

"Where have you been?" Slocum yelled, when he was still a city block away.

Sam cupped her hand at her ear, as if she couldn't quite hear, giving herself time to think.

"Where were you?" Slocum asked. "If Jake hadn't said he knew where to find you"—Slocum smirked, glad to have proven Jake wrong—"your Dad would have sent out a search party."

Sam still didn't answer, because she was distracted. With their horses just feet apart, Sam saw Slocum's big palomino chew at his bit. Foam had gathered at the corners of his mouth, and he rolled his eyes.

"This is pretty rough country for a newcomer," Slocum added.

"I was born here, Mr. Slocum."

"So, where have you been?" Slocum squinted past her, but Sam didn't turn to see if the silver stallion had followed.

If he had, she'd chase him away herself. The Phantom was one trophy Slocum would never have.

"I woke up and decided to go for a ride," she said. That much was true. She hadn't mentioned *where* she'd awakened.

Sam's chin lifted as she waited.

"No one came to wake me for the four o'clock shift," Slocum said. He sized her up, then looked Ace over. "I think you were out looking for trouble."

"Sorry, sir." Sam shrugged. "I wasn't looking for anything but the way back to camp."

Slocum shook his head. "You expect me to believe that?"

Why was Slocum so suspicious? Sam wondered. Unless he was stalking the stallion by night, he couldn't know the Phantom had come to her. She wouldn't give Slocum any reason to think such a thing.

"I'm a lousy liar. Ask my dad." Sam looked away from Slocum as another rider came toward them at an easy lope. "Or ask Jake."

Sam watched Jake approach. Her friend rode with a fluid grace she could only admire. If she rode for another fifty years, she wouldn't look that natural on a horse.

Jake's mount slowed, stopped. Jake flashed her a look that said she had some explaining to do.

"Morning, Sam," he said. His voice was lazy.

"She says she was just out for a ride," Slocum sounded like a tattletale.

"That's pretty much what I figured," Jake said.

"The way she was speaking up for mustangs the other night, I figured she went looking for some," Slocum said.

Sam's heart hammered so hard, she could feel it in her throat.

Slocum winked at Jake. "Better bait than hay with sweet molasses, that's how young girls work on horses."

"You sure that's not with unicorns?" Jake asked without cracking a smile.

"I hope Gram wasn't worried," Sam blurted.

"No problem. Grace put some biscuits aside for your breakfast. I told Wyatt I'd get you a fresh horse and help you catch up with the herd."

Jake's expression didn't change. His high cheekbones and hard jaw might have been carved of redwood, but the heat in his eyes told Sam that Dad had taken lots of convincing.

Slocum looked between the two as if he expected an argument. Sam knew that might come later, in private, but not in front of Slocum, who seemed to yearn for division between then.

When nothing happened, Slocum gave a disgusted grunt.

"I'm headed back. You two can ride in together." Slocum jabbed ornate spurs at the palomino's sides and galloped away.

"No reason to run," Jake yelled after Slocum, then mused to himself. "He's just the sort who'll cuss his horse if it steps in a ground squirrel hole."

Sam and Jake sat in silence, broken only by the creak of saddle leather.

"Ever hear your dad call me a good tracker?" Jake asked, finally.

He stared off at the horizon. Sam knew Jake wasn't bragging, just hinting he knew the truth, and giving her a chance to confess.

"He says you're a *world-class* tracker," Sam admitted.

"I was ten when I trailed Smoke to a wild bunch."

"I know," Sam said.

"And you remember Buck Henry."

"Sure." Sam swallowed hard.

Buck Henry was a hermit who'd broken into Jake's dad's meat house and made it look like the work of a bear. Only Jake hadn't been fooled. He'd trailed Henry to his mountain cabin and knocked on the door before the man could fry a single stolen steak.

"I don't suppose you know about the cattle thieves." This time Jake gave her a quick, sideways glance.

"Dad told me you were in Darton, after school one day," Sam said, "and identified tire prints from a truck that had driven off with some of our stock. You got them arrested." Sam urged Ace toward camp. "So, what's your point, Jake?"

She wouldn't lie to him, but she wouldn't give away the Phantom's hiding place, either.

"You think I don't know what happened?" Jake asked.

"I think that if you bothered to look at our tracks, you know exactly what happened," Sam snapped.

For Jake, it would be as if she'd left a note saying she'd galloped off with a wild horse.

"You want to talk about it?" Jake pulled his fingers through his rein ends.

"Not now," Sam answered.

"That's what I figured, but there's two things I need to tell you. First, if you've seen the Phantom, you know he has a scar on his neck. Slocum put it there."

Sam caught her breath and felt dizzy. "How?"

"Slocum roped him from the back of a moving truck. The other end of the rope was tied to a barrel full of hardened cement."

Sam covered her lips to keep a gasp inside. She

thought of her colt's delicate neck, of the concrete snubbing him to a stop.

"He couldn't get away, but he tried, flinging himself against the rope, even though it was choking him."

Sam could almost hear the echo of the stallion's terrified scream.

"But Slocum got greedy. He left Phantom fighting the barrel, and went after an Appaloosa mare running with the herd. By the time he got back, the Phantom was gone."

Sam thanked the instinct that had forced her out of the valley and away from the wild horses, before Slocum found her.

"Slocum asked me to track the Phantom." Jake gave a cold smile.

"But you didn't," Sam said.

"The blood drops would've made it easy and he offered me a couple hundred dollars," Jake said. "But I was too busy with school and stuff like that."

Sam wanted to tell Jake she was proud of him, but her mind kept replaying the stallion's screams. She rode beside Jake in silence, wondering what kind of monster would leave a wild horse alone and fighting, with every chance of breaking his neck.

Only the plastic corral and Gram's chuck wagon marked the place where camp had been. The herd of red and white cattle had moved on.

Before they rode in, Sam pulled Ace to a stop. "You said you needed to tell me two things. What's the other one?"

"Just this: you got hurt before because I wasn't watching you close enough." Jake raised his voice, refusing to let Sam contradict him. "This time, I'm going to stick to you like glue, Samantha Anne. Slocum's dead serious about catching that horse. He'll do whatever it takes—including using you as bait. But I'll do whatever I have to, to keep you safe."

Then Jake touched the brim of his hat and galloped away, before Sam had time to say a word.

Chapter Seven &

JAKE HAD A LOT of nerve. He'd "stick to her like glue," would he? In Sam's opinion, she'd proven herself halfway to being a cowgirl.

As she rode drag on Strawberry, Sam wondered why Jake still worried over a fall that had happened years ago. *She* thought about it because it had, after all, been her head Blackie had kicked as he escaped.

You got hurt because I wasn't watching you close enough, Jake had said. Had someone blamed Jake for her accident or was he blaming himself? Sam made a mental note to ask Gram.

Sam glanced up toward the front of the herd, but couldn't spot Jake's black hat and paint cow pony. After the drive, she and Jake must talk this out. She wanted a friend, not a watchdog.

They'd ridden for about an hour when Strawberry's gait changed. Had she picked up a rock? Sam stopped, ground-tied the mare and patted down her leg to lift a rear hoof and examine it.

In the quiet, wind rattled the buck brush and cattle calls drifted back to her. No rock was lodged in the hoof, and the stop had cost her only a couple minutes.

She gave Strawberry a pat before remounting. As Sam swung into the saddle, she glanced ahead to see if she'd have to hurry to catch up. That's when she noticed him.

Slocum had dropped back, too. Through the rolling dust, he sat watching her and scanning the open range.

Jake had said Slocum was using her as bait, but did Slocum expect the Phantom to come galloping to her side?

Sam waved at Slocum to let him know she'd noticed his spying. He didn't wave back, just let his horse walk on, as if he'd never stopped.

Maybe Jake wasn't being paranoid. Still, if he thought he could stand between her and the Phantom, just to keep Slocum away, Jake was dead wrong.

Sam pushed aside thoughts of Slocum and concentrated on tomorrow's crossing. They would be crossing the *playa*. Sam knew *playa* was Spanish for "beach." A thousand years ago, most of Nevada had been covered by ancient Lake Lahontan. Over centuries, the prehistoric waters had dwindled and a crust had formed over the muddy pools left behind.

The men had warned the crossing could be treacherous. This time last week, a risky crossing would have meant sprinting across Market Street ahead of a cable car or taxi. Tomorrow's crossing would be something new. Dallas had ordered an early stop today, so they could cross the *playa* in daylight.

When Dallas trotted back to join her at the rear of the herd, Sam grabbed her chance to ask questions.

Trying to act unconcerned, she wondered aloud if the crust always held up under the weight of the cattle.

"Not always," he said. "And the animals know it. They've got an instinct for when it's gonna break and any sound can cause them to stampede."

The crust could crack beneath a single hoof, he added, sending a cow and calf or horse and rider into the quicksand beneath.

"See you at camp," he said, then put his horse into a lope so he could catch the leaders.

Sam shuddered and wished the *playa* wasn't too huge to detour around.

The drive was over for the day. By the time Sam reached camp, the lead cows had made a muddy mess of the water hole. Some cattle had waded in up to their bellies. Others hung back, keeping calves apart from the crowd, until it was safe to drink.

Strawberry was thirsty, but she and the other horses weren't interested in a water hole packed with noisy cattle.

Sam didn't know Jake was behind her until his voice startled her.

"There's a pond up the hill where the mustangs drink," he said. "Let's take the horses up there, after dinner."

"Quit stalking me," Sam snapped at him.

Jake rode past, but he glanced back over his shoulder and smiled. Though she didn't catch all he said, Sam heard the words, "like glue."

She couldn't imagine a more annoying friend.

After chili, cornbread, and a mound of green salad, Sam didn't feel like riding to the mustangs' water hole. Just lifting a saddle onto a horse's back seemed like work.

Jake looked her way and her weariness must have shown.

"Forget it. They can drink down here," Jake said. "You didn't sleep much last night, what with night-hawking and all."

Sam was tempted, until she thought of the two bottles of clear, cold water she'd chugged with dinner. The horses had worked a lot harder than she, and only had a few sips of muddy water.

Dallas must have seen her hesitation. "Sam, you go on ahead to bed and catch up on your sleep," he said. "I'll get one of the boys to help Jake."

One of the boys. Something in Sam growled at Dallas's offer. His words were like a dare, and

Jake was about to laugh.

"Give me five minutes and I'll meet you at the corral," she told Jake, then turned to the pot suspended over the campfire. "Gram, do you mind if I take a little of this before it turns into dishwater?"

"Help yourself, dear," Gram said.

Sam washed her face, then considered her reflection in the little mirror Gram had hung on the back of the chuck wagon.

Her sunburned cheeks felt worse than they looked, but blowing dust and short hours of sleep showed in her bloodshot eyes. Sam longed for some lip balm and she wished she hadn't chopped off her hair. Braiding it might have made her feel tidy. She leaned close to the mirror and fluffed her fingers through her bangs.

It sure was a lot of trouble, proving she was tough enough to belong.

Finally, Sam tucked her hair behind her ears.

"Best I can do," Sam said as Gram's reflection appeared alongside hers.

"You look like a cowgirl, and that's all the horses care about." Gram kissed her cheek, then stood back as if she had more to say. "I know Jake gets on your nerves, sometimes."

"It's worse than that." When Sam noticed she'd put her hands on her hips, she let them slide off. "He either ignores me or acts like a mother hen."

"Don't you think that's natural? After your

accident?" Gram asked.

"I don't know what it is, Gram." Sam leaned over and whispered, loudly, "But he's driving me nuts!"

Sam waved good-bye and took two minutes to rummage through the tent for her black sweater. No luck. She jogged to the corral and arrived as Jake rode by, herding most of the saddle horses in front of him.

"I left Ace and Strawberry for you," he said. "Just take the path up that ridge."

His gesture was easy to follow, and Sam had no doubt she could handle the last two horses.

After a lazy day just moving with the remuda, Ace rushed the fence, seeming glad to see her.

"Hi, good boy," she said, stroking the velvety nose he thrust over the fence. Ace nodded until his forelock uncovered the white star high on his forehead and she rubbed that, too.

Sam considered the short ride up the ridge and decided to ride him bareback, while she led Strawberry.

Jake had said he'd taken all the other horses, but as she entered the corral, Sam noticed a third horse tied nearby, at the same time that she smelled cigarette smoke.

The brown Thoroughbred had the long legs and deep chest of a steeplechaser. Double sets of saddlebags hung from his saddle and the man drawing his cinch tight was Linc Slocum.

Everything about the horse and saddle made Sam

nervous. She bridled Ace, thinking that Slocum was prepared for more than nighthawking. Just the same, Sam returned Slocum's wave, before leading Ace from the corral.

"I'm giving you a break from that heavy saddle," Sam muttered as she vaulted onto Ace's back. "Don't dump me and make me look bad."

Aunt Sue would have said the gelding acted sweet as a lamb. As he plodded up the trail, Sam watched the sky. Dark clouds hung over an amazing sunset. Often, over the past two years, Aunt Sue had coaxed her to watch San Francisco Bay turn gold as it swallowed the setting sun. The scene was always nice, but for Sam fell far short of entertainment.

Today, Sam had seen the sun rise and set. No one had prompted her to watch. The fiery tangerine color flooding the desert foothills made Sam understand Aunt Sue's enjoyment.

Then she heard him. Sam knew, even before the horses' ears pricked forward, that the Phantom had returned. His nicker floated around her like the words to a secret song.

"Where is he, Ace?" Sam whispered. "Where?" She twisted at the waist, scanning every rise and dip of the land around her.

Somewhere, hooves skittered on rock. Sam urged Ace and Strawberry up the trail for a better view, but still there was nothing, except Slocum's shout.

"I knew it!" His words carried from below.

No! Slocum must have spotted the stallion first. His Thoroughbred leaped into action, covering yards of desert, stretched low as a greyhound.

Ace pulled at the bit and danced in place, eager to join the chase, but Sam kept him reined in. Still she saw nothing.

"You okay?" Jake was suddenly there on foot. He grabbed her reins near the bit and gave a tug to make Ace settle.

"I'm fine, but Slocum—"

Jake pointed and Sam's eyes followed. The Phantom was leading the Thoroughbred across the desert.

A pale wisp, he teased Slocum's mount. Phantom let the Thoroughbred draw close enough that he must feel the Thoroughbred's breath on his tail. Then the stallion jumped a clump of sagebrush and doubled back with impossible agility.

More ghost than horse, the mustang disappeared in the middle of a hillside with Slocum still thundering after him.

Sam told herself everything would be fine. The Phantom would escape. But that night in her dreams, she saw the stallion dashing through snow drifts, past a candy-cane North Pole, while Slocum followed in a sleigh, face fringed with a beard of ice.

Thunder woke Sam before dawn. She wriggled deeper in her sleeping bag and listened to the lowing of restless cattle. Raindrops pattered on the canvas tent. In the dimness, she saw Gram's bed, neatly tied in a roll.

Dallas called, "Boots on the ground, we're burnin' daylight."

"*What* daylight?" Jake's voice came from somewhere nearby. His spurs chimed and a horse snorted its bad mood as its hooves sucked across wet ground.

Sam heard bacon sizzling.

Moving like an inchworm, she scooted to the tent flap and pulled it back.

"Psst," she whispered.

Jake heard her over the hissing curtain of rain, and stopped.

"Is Slocum back?" she asked him.

Rain dripped off Jake's black hat brim as he shook his head and kept riding.

Slocum had been out all night, after the Phantom.

Sam pulled on her jeans. Four days of riding had finally caught up with her. She ached all over and the contortions required to tug up her socks made Sam bite her lip against a whimper.

Dad was waiting by the campfire. He gave her a wink and a yellow slicker. Once she'd struggled into the raincoat, he offered her a warm pottery mug. Steam curled up from the creamy combination of cocoa and coffee and Sam sighed with delight.

The cold sneaking between her upturned collar and pulled down hat made the hot drink taste even better.

Pepper approached the other side of the fire and rubbed his hands together. He wore a long duster which must be oiled, because the water beaded on it.

The bad weather had put him in a playful mood.

"Great day for crossin' the *playa*," Pepper said, with a wicked grin. "Rain pourin' down from on high and water bubblin' up underfoot."

"Is it really?" Sam asked. She tried to look out of camp, past the herd, to the *playa*.

"You bet. Think of a hard-boiled egg. Y'know how you give it a whack so you can peel off the shell?" Pepper asked, and Sam nodded. "Well, the *playa*'s like that. Little cracks all over the place, with quicksand underneath, just waiting to suck in your horse's hoof and pull you down, down, down."

As Pepper's voice quavered into the creepy tone you'd use to scare a child, Sam knew she'd been had.

"Hey, you don't want to go scaring a dude like that."

Dude? Sam looked up to see which of Slocum's cowboys the words had come from. She thought it had been Flick. Not that it mattered. They were all laughing at her.

"Quicksand doesn't suck you under," Dad said, sipping at his coffee, looking patient. "It's just a thick combination of sand and water. It doesn't have a mind of its own."

"I know," Sam said, but she didn't.

"The main thing's to keep the herd together and

quiet. Don't do anything to spook 'em."

Dad glanced at her, confirming that she knew what he meant. Cattle, horses, even people got edgy during a storm. The least little thing could spook them into doing something stupid.

"If a cow does go through," Dad added, "we can rope her and pull her out."

Sam hoped he was right, but she remembered an adventure movie in which the villain had died struggling in quicksand. The last shot had shown his hat, sitting on the surface of the gritty ooze. But she didn't bring that up.

"Think you all have time to quit joshing and move some cows?" Dallas asked.

The men mounted up. Sam gave Gram a stiff smile and went off to get Ace. She imagined the earth cracking and a black goo swallowing her without a trace.

As always, Jake read her mind. "You can swim right out of it," he said, quietly. "If you don't panic."

"You take care of your little girlfriend, now." Flick grinned at Jake. "Even if they have good bloodlines, dudes scare real easy."

Sam ignored Flick, just like she would any smart-mouthed jerk at school.

"Sam's no dude," Jake responded. Sam felt herself relax before he added, "More of a *dudette*, I'd say."

Jake wheeled Witch away from the other riders, away from Sam. That was a good thing, too, Sam thought as Witch carried Jake splashing away into the gray morning. She still had an empty mug in her hand and she could barely suppress the urge to fling it at Jake's head.

Stop. Go. Stop. Go. All morning they followed the cautious cattle through the rain, never pushing, just watching.

Dallas hadn't asked her to ride drag today. He assigned her to ride on the right side of the herd. She knew better than to ask why.

Thunder rumbled overhead and a cold wind blew.

Sam hunched her shoulders inside her slicker and pulled her brown Stetson lower on her brow. Her cheeks were cold, but rubbing them with her gloved hand didn't help.

"Hey dudette, how's it goin'?" Pepper called from the other side of the herd. He sounded good-natured, but Sam didn't answer.

Whether it was Pepper's shout, the thunder, or her bovine imagination, a big brindle cow wearing Slocum's brand spooked. She bolted away from the herd, just yards in front of Ace.

Ace tensed to follow, to gallop after the cow and return her to the herd. Sam clapped her heels to the gelding's sides and let him fly off in pursuit.

Dudette, am I? Sam stayed loose in the saddle, as Jake had told her to do when riding a cutting horse. But the brindle cow didn't want to go back.

"Hey!" Sam shouted. No way was this cow going to slip past her. Holding her reins in one hand, Sam snatched off her hat and flapped it at the cow, trying to scare her back toward the herd.

Rolling her eyes white, the cow bowled past Ace with a bellow.

Humiliation made Sam glance back to see if any of the cowboys had noticed her failure.

What she saw made her sick.

Chapter Eight &

ℱRIGHTENED BY THE BRINDLE cow's bellows, the rest of the herd split off in all directions. Some trotted with their heads held high, ears swivelling in confusion. Others galloped, eyes rolled white. Big red bodies slammed each other as the cattle ignored everything but fear. Though the cowboys kept their horses at a walk, trying to regather cattle without scaring them even more, Sam knew what had happened. She'd caused a stampede.

Once she returned the brindle cow to what remained of the herd, Sam rode at the edge of the restless bunch. She surveyed the *playa*, hoping she'd see no animals sunk in quicksand.

What she did see was Jake, shepherding about thirty head her way.

Sam braced herself, but Jake didn't yell, didn't accuse, didn't even give her a hard look. He kept his eyes on the herd.

Somehow, that was worse.

"Jake, I was stupid," she said. "I was trying to show off, to prove I knew what I was doing, and I did just the opposite. I moved too fast. I didn't think—"

Jake's mouth was set in a hard line as he nodded. Agreeing. He sent Witch off at a gentle jog after two cows with calves.

It took the experienced cowboys about twenty minutes to regather the herd, but to Sam it felt like hours.

Stupid, stupid, stupid. So the cowboys had joked with her. So they'd called her names. Big deal. Now her inexperienced look-at-me action had ruined everything. She had acted just like a dude.

The men riding around her, even Dad, would forget she'd ridden out Ace's bucking fits. They'd forget she'd risen from her warm sleeping bag to nighthawk at midnight. They'd forget she'd helped take the horses to water, even when she was bone tired.

Rain pounded down, bouncing up like popcorn from the cows' backs. When she glanced away at a squishing sound, Sam saw Dad riding toward her on Banjo.

As he stopped beside her, Sam drew Ace to a halt.

"What happened?" Dad asked.

Sam took a breath. She couldn't deny the stampede had been her fault, but she could keep herself from crying. She cleared her throat and leaned forward, pretending to straighten the headstall behind Ace's ears.

"A cow spooked and broke from the herd. I let Ace go after her." Sam bit her lower lip, then corrected herself. "I made him go after her."

Dad put Banjo into a walk and shook his head.

"That wouldn't do it. It must have been something else." He gave her a sympathetic smile. "It wasn't your fault."

It would be easy to accept his mistake, but it wouldn't be right.

"I'm pretty sure it was me," she said. "I yelled at the cow and flapped my hat in her face."

Dad gave an astonished laugh, which did not sound amused. "That'd do it, all right."

As they rode, Sam waited for Dad to say something else. Up ahead, Ross tucked his bandanna inside his slicker, as if the sight of its ends blowing in the wind could spook the cattle. Sam did the same.

"No harm done, this time." Dad's sober look said there'd better not be a next time. "No legs broken or calves lost, far as I can tell."

"I'll stop being so sensitive," Sam said.

Dad nodded. "Good. They don't joke with folks they don't like. They just ignore them."

Sam wondered if Dad was referring to Slocum, whose own cowboys rarely spoke to him.

"I'm sending a couple riders forward to the chuck wagon to help your grandmother set up camp," Dad continued. "In this wind, the tents will be more than one person can handle. We'll need to trench around them, too, so rain doesn't flood us out of our beds. Do you want to go?"

Dad was offering her a chance to escape. Unlike the cowboys, Gram wouldn't fix her with eyes that accused her of causing extra work. On the other hand, riding away seemed a lot like surrender.

"Not unless you need me to go," Sam said. "I'll probably be living this down 'til I'm fifty years old, right?"

"Possible," Dad said. "But there's always a chance they'll forget. You might save Flick when he's treed by a grizzly."

Sam savored the image a minute, then cocked her head to see her father's face under his hat's broad brim. "There aren't any grizzlies around here," Sam said.

"You're learning." He laughed, then squinted toward a rider coming up from behind the herd.

As he drew close, Sam saw Pepper's dun horse was black with exertion.

"Boss," Pepper said, a little breathless himself, "we got some trouble."

Dad sent the herd on with the other hands, but Jake accompanied Sam and Dad as Pepper led them to the trouble.

A tiny calf was trapped in a mire of quicksand.

His bleating had turned gruff, as if he had a sore throat from calling his mother.

"Where's your mama, little guy?" Dad's voice was gentle, but he kept his distance. "Sam, stay back." Dad held out his arm as if stopping traffic. "This crust is thin."

Lunging to escape the quicksand, the calf had cleared an area big as a bathtub. If his struggles had done that, the desert floor certainly wouldn't hold a horse.

Dad's rope whirred through the air and settled. The lariat looked huge around the calf's neck.

"Better make this quick," Dad said, then spurred Banjo into a jump forward.

Instead of letting himself be dragged free, the calf tried to swim. His flailing forelegs broke through the crust again and again.

Dad backed Banjo and let the rope go slack.

"If I could get a loop past his front legs, around his whole front end, he'd slide right out," Dad said.

But that wasn't going to happen. They could all see that.

Weak with fatigue, the calf gave a cranky bawl, then pillowed his head on the quicksand, sinking until his neck and the rope were submerged.

Jake rode a wide circle around the calf. "It's not like a mom to walk away, unless she thought he was—" Jake shrugged.

Dead. Sam gazed at the calf's closed eyelids and

white eyelashes. The little animal was helpless.

Both Jake and Dad looked as if they'd given up hope. She knew orphan calves required lots of time and trouble. Sam also knew the whole summer stretched ahead of her. She could help.

"If we can get him out, I'll bottle-feed him," Sam offered.

Dad gave her a sad smile. "Even then, he couldn't keep up with the herd."

"I'll carry him across my saddle."

"Honey, sometimes you lose one. It's hard, but you'll come to grips with it, living out here."

Looking thoughtful, but a little hesitant to offer advice to his boss, Pepper said, "I know what we'd do if he'd fallen through the ice."

Sam's pulse pounded fast. Years of cold had made Pepper leave northern Idaho. She'd bet he knew all about ice rescues.

"Go ahead," Dad encouraged him.

"The lightest one of us goes flat on the ice, or the crust, I guess, and kind of wiggles toward the opening. The idea is to keep the weight distributed over as broad an area as possible. You can't do that on a horse, or walking, but spread-eagled on your belly, it works." Pepper looked away from the calf to Sam. "We'd probably want a rope around her waist, just in case."

Her waist. Sam waited for Dad to protest that the scheme was too dangerous. When he didn't, she felt a little dizzy.

"Then," Pepper continued, "she'd get a good grip on the calf and we'd pull 'em out."

Dusk and rain clouds grayed the desert all around. The quicksand looked thick and clammy. A coyote called, trying to gather friends to go hunting. Sam shivered at the lonely sound.

"Let's do it," Sam said.

Trying to look confident, she dismounted and tossed Ace's reins toward Jake.

He caught them, but flashed a questioning look at her dad. "Wyatt?"

It was the first time she'd heard Jake address Dad by his first name. Some man-to-man protectiveness in Jake's tone irritated Sam.

"It's up to Sam," Dad said.

Sam liked being her own boss. For the last year, she'd argued with Aunt Sue over whether she was mature enough to make her own decisions. Right this minute, though, she wished Dad had taken charge.

"Shoot, he's half-dead already." Jake sounded disgusted, but he looked troubled. And paler than she'd ever seen him. "There's no branded mama around. Why, there's no telling if he's even a River Bend calf. He could be Slocum's."

"Of course, I'll do it." Sam warmed her palms against the front of her jeans. Jake's worry actually made her feel stronger.

"You're not going to let me drown," she explained

to Jake. "And the calf's not going to hurt me. I'm going to hold onto that baby so tight that even if you have to drag me to San Francisco, he won't get loose."

Jake looked away, fed up with her.

Within five minutes, Dad's rope was tight around her waist and Sam lay on the surprisingly warm desert floor. She inched her way toward the calf. He was wide awake, now, and bucking out of her reach.

"It's okay little guy. I won't hurt you."

Sam was dimly aware of the men barking advice, but her world had narrowed to the calf bawling and bucking in front of her.

"How about some nice warm milk," she crooned.

The calf's ears fluttered her way. Then she pounced. *Now.* She hunched her shoulders forward. Keeping her legs still, Sam plunged her arms through the quicksand. It felt like cold oatmeal. She caught the calf in a bear hug.

Maaaaa, maaaaa.

She could swear the calf called for his mother, but Sam held tight. His front legs tap-danced against her chest. The rope jerked her middle up, then they began to slide backward. Fast.

And then she stopped.

"You can let go. Sam, let go!" Jake squatted beside her, prying loose the arms she'd locked around the calf.

By the time Sam wriggled free of Dad's rope, she noticed Jake had a smear of blood on his cheek.

"What happened?" she asked.

"Your little buddy butted him in the nose," Dad said. He gathered his rope in, fastening it in a loop on his saddle.

Sam felt happy. She felt shaky. And when Pepper helped her balance the calf across her saddle to ride back into camp, she felt proud.

That night, Sam shrugged off the cowboys' jokes about the stampede. She was too busy trying to save the calf's life.

For a while the calf remained limp, then thrashed and fought as Sam introduced the bottle Gram had fixed.

"Come on, little guy," Sam grunted.

She knew Pepper had stopped to watch her, but she didn't look up, even when he said, "Maybe she's mad 'cause you're calling her a guy. That little critter's a female."

Sam didn't care. She only knew that for an animal no bigger than a dog, the calf was incredibly strong. The red rope-burn around Sam's waist stung as she tried to drip milk past the calf's tightly shut pink lips. By the time the calf figured out she wanted the milk, Sam's arm muscles had stretched like rubber bands and her hands trembled.

Once the calf fell asleep beside her, Sam slurped down the soup Gram made her eat. She sighed, feeling better, and looked around. The campfire crackled orange and bright against the darkness. Except for Gram, she was alone.

"Time for bed." Gram untied her apron and yawned.

"I can't leave her," Sam said. "Can I sleep out here?"

"It's not good for either one of you, but your dad already said you could." Gram tsked her tongue. "You'll probably get sick, but we're almost home. You'll be sleeping in your own bed tomorrow night."

Gram was doing a good job of talking herself into it, so Sam didn't say a word except "thank you" when Gram brought out her sleeping bag.

The calf lay beside Sam, exhausted. Her thin eyelids twitched. What did calves dream of?

Sam knew that if she dozed, she'd dream of the Phantom.

Today she'd had a rope around her middle. Through her clothes, it had sawed a sore abrasion, even though Dad had been quick and gentle. She thought of the Phantom, caught by a rope and that barrel of cement. There'd been no worry over his suffering and pain.

Now Slocum was after him again.

Sam stroked the calf's fur and tried to think of

something else. The little animal had grown used to her touch so quickly, she didn't even wake.

Sam stared into the satiny orange flames of the campfire. She thought back to how Pepper had suggested her for a dangerous job and Dad had let her make up her own mind. Sam looked down at her hands and wondered if she'd ever get the dirt out from under her fingernails.

She hadn't seen Jake since they'd returned to camp. She remembered his gentle firmness, removing her arms from the calf's neck. There'd been a smear of blood on Jake's cheek.

What was it Dad had said? Oh yeah, *Your little buddy butted him in the nose.*

Sam petted the calf some more. "How about if I name you Buddy? I don't see why it couldn't be a girl's name, do you?"

Since the calf made no protest, Sam settled down to rest. The tendons holding her head up relaxed.

She was almost asleep when she heard a disturbance at the corral. Hooves churned and horses nickered in greeting.

At the edge of the firelight, a rider appeared.

Slocum slumped on the brown Thoroughbred, looking around. Sam was pretty sure he didn't see her, there in the shadow of the chuck wagon. Sam didn't move, didn't say a word.

Slocum had returned empty-handed.

Sam felt a quick surge of pleasure, until Slocum

hauled on his reins, turning the Thoroughbred. In the firelight, Sam saw dried foam around the horse's bit. Behind his cinch, long bloody gouges had been raked by Slocum's spurs.

Chapter Nine ∾

"No one likes housework, young lady," said Gram. "That's why TV commercials have singing scrub bubbles and dancing toilet brushes."

Gram stood with her hands on her hips. She'd caught Sam trying to slip out the front door on cleaning day. That had not put Gram in a good mood.

Sam had no chance to offer an excuse. Gram kept talking.

"I'm giving you a choice. Stay indoors and help me, or hightail it out to the barn and clean out a winter's worth of straw and manure."

Mentally, Sam compared the smell of ammonia and glass cleaner with the scents of a summer barn. Kind of a toss-up. Though it was cool indoors and hot outside, in the barn she'd have Buddy for company. She'd be in a better mood than Gram.

Sam rubbed her eyes. This would teach her to sleep in.

Each night since they'd been home from the drive, she'd crept out of bed about midnight and waited, watching by moonlight for the Phantom. If she'd awakened early, she'd have ridden out with the cowboys. Dad, Pepper, and Ross hated riding the fence line and mending breaks the cattle might escape through, but Sam knew it was more fun than housework.

Jake couldn't offer any distraction, either. He'd stayed home to help his dad with an irrigation problem. To Sam, even standing knee-deep in water sounded like heaven.

"Take your pick." Gram tapped her foot.

"The barn," Sam said and made a run for it.

Sam stabbed a pitchfork under a dusty layer of straw, and lifted.

Blaze, the ranch dog, lay in the shade of the barn watching. As Sam dropped the straw into the wheelbarrow, Blaze sneezed.

Sam stopped, pushing back the locks of hair that curved on her cheeks as her short cut began to grow out. She'd been working for an hour, and the chore wasn't as gross as she'd feared. Still, the most exciting part of ranching was over for this year.

The cattle drive had been the high point and this was, she hoped, the low point.

Once again, Sam filled the wheelbarrow and rolled it out into the sunshine. Buddy did her best to make the job fun, frolicking beside Sam as she passed the corrals and dumped the dried straw and manure on a growing hill. Instead of buying garden fertilizer, Gram used this stuff.

After just a few days at the ranch, Buddy was peppy and healthy. She twirled her tail in a corkscrew, then made little hip-hop bucks. She was pretty happy for an orphan.

"And pretty lucky," Sam told her. Slocum hadn't claimed Buddy and Dad hadn't mentioned turning the calf out with the beef cattle. "Stay runty and maybe you can spend your life as a pet," Sam added.

Buddy spooked and ran around to Sam's other side, ears cupped toward the pasture. Blaze got to his feet. Ears alert, he made an inquiring noise deep in his throat. Ace and a few other horses stopped grazing. They stood statue-still, attention aimed toward the river.

Chills sprinkled over Sam's scalp and down her shoulders. The Phantom wouldn't come to the ranch in the daylight, but she'd never seen the other horses act this way, except when he did.

Sam scanned the wild side of the river, but saw nothing. She was imagining things. Why would the stallion come back again?

Sam rolled the wheelbarrow back to the barn and bent to her task. She didn't *want* to give up hope the stallion would return, that was all.

She kept after her work, back and forth from the

barn. All the while, she imagined the stallion watching. He wasn't, of course. The last time he'd come to her, Slocum had chased him day and night. Had his lungs burned? Had he wondered why one of his own kind joined a man to hunt him? And before that, when Slocum ripped his flesh with ropes and weights, what had the Phantom thought, under those crashing waves of panic?

Men had done nothing but hurt him.

Sam leaned the pitchfork against the barn wall and appreciated the clean barn and stall she'd tidied for Buddy. Then she heard a splash. Sam turned and looked out the wide barn doors. Against all logic, her horse had returned anyway.

Sam walked from the barn. She moved smoothly, reaching out to the stallion with her thoughts. *I'll never hurt you.*

The horse gleamed like polished ivory. His hide glimmered at each flex of muscles as he lifted his knees through the silver sluice of water. Even when Sam reached the bridge, he kept coming, fording the deepest part of the river with his broad chest.

Sam's heart threatened to beat free of her own chest.

"Zanzibar," she whispered as the stallion looked left and right, as if he'd cross the river and walk right up to her.

He shouldn't. She wouldn't hurt him, of course, but she was human. Humans would always want to capture and cage an animal as beautiful as Zanzibar. He shouldn't trust her.

And yet he swam. Head surging forward, nostrils distended to show pink inside, he came to her. Sam thought of a myth she'd studied in English class. Poseidon the ocean god had driven horses whose white manes blew back on the wave crests.

River Bend might be just a small ranch in a desert state, but Zanzibar was a stallion fit for a god.

His hooves grazed river rock and he stopped, still knee-deep in water. For a minute, he looked away, but one ear turned in Sam's direction. Each second, she thought he'd bolt, but he didn't. He blew through his lips, opening his mouth as if to speak, then closing it, as if he were too shy.

Sam tried to understand. Instead of reaching out to the stallion with her mind, she used her heart. He remembered the ranch, but how did his equine mind remember her?

The stallion lowered his muzzle almost to the water. Instead of drinking, he uttered a low rumble that begged her to reply.

"I took care of you, Zanzibar. When you were a foal and just weaned from your mom, I stayed with you, didn't I, boy?"

The stallion kept his head low, but the angle of his ears told Sam to keep talking.

"Remember that thunderstorm when you were a yearling? It shook the barn walls and Dad let me stay, petting you all night until my fingers were stiff. I fell asleep and missed the school bus. Dad said when he came into the barn, you were standing over me like a big guard dog. So, I guess you took care of me, too."

He was a stallion now, an adult. What help could she give, that he couldn't get from his herd?

Her silence broke the spell. Zanzibar had become the Phantom once more. The stallion backed three splashing steps away, then lowered into the current, silver dapples glinting as he struck out for the other shore.

What did the stallion want? He had a lush valley full of mares and foals. They were his family. She could offer him nothing but captivity. Even if Jake helped her use gentle ways to bring the stallion in, he'd hate her for it.

Sam stared at the hills long after the horse vanished. Half of her wanted to hug this secret close. Half of her wanted to tell Jake.

Buddy nuzzled her hand, then licked her palm with a long tongue, reminding her it was time to eat.

They returned to the barn where Sam had stowed a full bottle. The calf tugged at the nipple. Her eyes rolled back and her tail switched in pure delight. Sam remembered when helping Zanzibar had been this simple.

Things had changed so much in two years. Now Sam didn't know what to do.

◖◯◗

The next morning Sam ran out to the barn before breakfast. She fed Buddy and turned her into a pasture adjoining the barn. The calf had the grassy enclosure to herself. Though she looked small out there alone, the calf would have a good time until it was time to go back to the barn for a midday bottle.

Sam went back to the house and washed her hands.

"Can I help you with anything, Gram?" she asked.

If Gram answered, Sam didn't notice. What she did hear was Jake's spurs chiming before he sauntered through the kitchen door.

"You're in for the time of your life, Samantha." Jake took his hat from fresh-washed hair and snatched a piece of bacon from the plate Gram placed on the table. "Wyatt's going to let me drive his truck up to the mustang corrals at Willow Springs."

"The mustang corrals?" Sam felt excited and worried all at once.

"Willow Springs is where the BLM holds wild horses until they're adopted," Jake explained. "And you," Jake used his bacon like a scepter, "get to come along."

"Lucky me," Sam said. She wasn't sure she liked the BLM, because they took wild horses off the range, and she was half afraid Jake would act overprotective around even captive mustangs.

Jake ignored her sarcasm and added, "'Course,

Wyatt's coming, too, since I only have my learner's permit."

Sam drained the rest of her orange juice and watched Jake. Should she tell him about the Phantom? Maybe when no one else was around.

"You are lucky," Gram told her. "Wyatt doesn't have much use for the Bureau of Land Management." Gram glanced over as the door opened to show Dad stamping off his boots. "You'd think visiting their corrals was paying a call on the Devil himself."

"Them talking about raising grazing fees again isn't improving my attitude," Dad said. He looked over Gram's shoulder as she flipped two pancakes at once. He licked his lips, then added, "I can rein in my tongue long enough to take Sam up there. She's been a big help at home, while we've been riding fence."

Sam felt a burst of pleasure at the compliment. Dad was taking a day off from ranch chores just for her.

"Thanks, Dad," Sam said.

"You've earned it," Dad's voice said he wouldn't tolerate any sentiment. "Let's just hope Jake gets us there in one piece."

Gram handed him a cup of coffee. "I wondered if you were ever coming in," she said. "I thought I was going to have to feed these pancakes to the dog."

Outside, Blaze thumped his tail in appreciation, but Sam wondered why Gram sounded cranky. She'd just cooked those pancakes, so they weren't the real problem.

For two days in a row Gram had acted like this, and it was out of character. It had also made it impossible for Sam to ask Gram why Jake seemed to feel guilty over her accident.

"You be careful driving, Jake Ely, even backing out," Gram said. "I love that Buick, and if you hit it, your folks are footing the bill."

"Yes, ma'am," Jake said.

Jake looked puzzled by Gram's mood, too, and her attachment to the long yellow car, which must be two decades old.

Jake grabbed a chair, turned its back to face the table and straddled it.

"For heaven's sake, if you come to my table, sit right," Gram snapped.

"Yes, ma'am," Jake said again, but this time he sounded humble. He switched the chair to its proper position.

As Gram walked away, Jake's eyes asked Sam what was going on. Sam shrugged.

"BLM is pretty much done gathering horses for the year," Dad said. His sudden change of topic made Sam think he was trying to distract them from Gram's mood. "Those up at Willow Springs have been there a while."

"I'm glad they're done," Sam said. "But why?"

Dad sipped his coffee. "Usually, they won't gather when there are foals. Unless there's an emergency." Dad gestured toward the range. "I expect that bunch we saw them trying to round up the day you came home was in a real dry area and they didn't want 'em to go thirsty."

Jake continued Dad's explanation. "They use helicopters to drive them into traps. Then they truck them off the range, vaccinate and worm them and give them some vitamin-laced feed while they're waiting for adoption.

"Expensive stuff," Jake added. "Just putting a helicopter and pilot in the air has got to cost a thousand dollars."

"See where my grazing fees are going?" Dad grumbled.

Sam stared out the kitchen window, but she wasn't thinking of money. She imagined herself one of those horses. She heard the helicopter's racket overhead, felt herself slam into a corral and then a truck with other mustangs.

It must be terrifying, and yet she'd read that fewer mustangs were injured with helicopter herding than when men chased them on horseback.

Once more, Sam imagined herself a horse. Mustangs had no flying predators, but they knew ground attacks, from coyotes or cougars, meant blood and pain. Maybe that's why they considered the helicopters more of an annoyance than a threat.

"I've read about it," Sam said, slowly. "Does that mean we can just drive there, pick one out and bring it home?"

"Yep. If you've got a hundred and twenty-five dollars and a decent place to keep it," Dad said. "But don't bring your allowance, Sam. We're just window shopping."

Window shopping. Did that mean Dad might allow her to adopt a mustang later? There was only one mustang she wanted and the prospect made her heart beat faster.

"Might want to bring a sweater," Dad said, standing. "We might be back late." He turned to Gram, and added, "I talked with Dallas. He and the boys will take care of the evening chores. You just enjoy your day."

Sam didn't mention she had not been able to find her favorite black sweater since the cattle drive. That sounded careless. Now that Dad was treating her with respect, she didn't want him to change his mind.

As Dad followed Jake out the door, Sam hustled from table to sink, clearing plates. The curtains at the kitchen window moved in the early-morning breeze. Outside, Dad directed Jake in backing the truck.

"Come on back, come on," Dad said, motioning.

Sam smiled. Soon, Jake would be testing for his driver's license and Dad didn't miss an opportunity to teach him.

"Honey?" Gram put a hand on Sam's shoulder.

Sam turned. Gram's concerned expression reminded Sam of Gram's bad mood, but Gram reached a gentle hand to brush Sam's hair back from her eyes.

"What do you do, when you leave the house so late at night?"

Relief rushed through Sam.

"Nothing," Sam said. "When I get restless and can't sleep, I go out and listen to the coyotes, watch the horses in the pasture, and—" Sam told the truth. "I've seen some wild horses at the river."

Gram still looked skeptical.

"What did you *think* I was doing?"

"Never mind. Sorry I've been such a scold. I do that when I'm worried." Gram kissed Sam's cheek as Jake honked the truck horn outside. "You run along now, and have a good time."

Sam bolted out the front door and nearly collided with Dad.

"Gram talk to you?" Dad nodded toward the kitchen.

"Yes," Sam said. "But I don't know what about."

Dad gazed toward the river, looking embarrassed. "She thought you and Jake might be up to something."

"Jake," Sam said, slowly, "and me?" A blush heated her cheeks. *"Jake and me?"*

Why would Gram think she was sneaking out to meet Jake? Jake was like a brother. Almost.

"Guess she was way off base." Dad pulled at his hat brim.

"I was looking at the horses, Dad. It's the horses I missed while I was in San Francisco."

Dad smiled and opened the truck door. "It'll be a tight squeeze, but the three of us can fit. Slide on in," he said, indicating she'd be sandwiched between him and Jake in the truck cab. "And hang on tight."

Jake wasn't a bad driver, but the road to the Willow Springs Wild Horse Center made Sam appreciate her seat belt. The road's surface was like rock-hard corduroy and her teeth hammered together as they swooped through the high desert.

"Dad," Sam said, suddenly. "I forgot to ask Gram to give Buddy her bottle."

"I'm sure she'll think of it when that calf starts bawling." Dad must have thought she looked worried, because he added, "Gram's working out in her vegetable garden. That's not far from the barn. I think she'll hear Buddy just fine."

"Yeah." Sam bit her bottom lip. She didn't tell Dad she'd put Buddy out into the pasture, but since it was only a few yards farther from the garden, it probably wouldn't matter.

Suddenly the road slanted uphill.

"This next part's called Thread the Needle. We're almost there." Jake slowed slightly as the road narrowed, leaving just enough room for the truck as steep cliffs fell away on each side.

"Look hard and you'll see River Bend." Jake took a hand from the steering wheel to gesture down the cliff.

Sam didn't enjoy looking down, but she saw the river, glinting silver-blue in the distance. Between here and there, a maze of trails marked the steep hillside.

"Antelope paths," Dad said, his finger showing how they zigzagged through sagebrush and rocks.

Then the road slanted downhill and the Willow Springs Center was spread before them. To Sam, it looked like a patchwork quilt with pipe fencing for stitching.

Sam's stomach tightened as they drove slowly past the pens. On her right horses moved away from the fences. On her left stood an office building and a parking lot for three white trucks with "U.S. Government" stenciled on their doors. Ahead, horses waited as a huge bearded man broke open bales of hay.

Why did she feel nervous, when everything seemed normal? The pens looked clean. The horses weren't crowded. A hill in each corral insured rain would run off before the mustangs stood in deep mud. Nothing was wrong.

Sam noticed two mares standing head-to-tail, eyes half closed as their tails swished flies from each others' faces. Then she recognized what was wrong. These "wild" horses looked tame.

A door slammed and a trim red-haired woman in a crisp khaki uniform left the office building.

"Hey," she called to a bespectacled man standing at a corral with a clipboard. "We have thirty head coming in from the Calico Range."

"Ready," he answered, gesturing toward three empty corrals.

Sam heard Jake draw a breath. Clearly he'd listened, too. Something the two BLM officials had said surprised him.

"What is it?" Sam asked.

Jake lifted one shoulder in a shrug.

"Since our cattle drive ran right along the Calico Mountains," Dad said, "I suppose he's thinking the wild band you two saw has been trapped. Is that it, Jake?"

Sam's mind swarmed with images of the Phantom running across the range, with Slocum in pursuit.

"Could be," Jake said, but before he went on, the red-haired woman interrupted.

"Hello," she said. "Are you thinking about adopting a wild horse?"

Now that the woman stood closer, Sam saw her name tag read "B. Olson." She had freckles. The sun lines around her blue eyes said she spent more time outside than in the beige office building.

"Just looking," Dad said.

The woman glanced away to take in the truck's Nevada license plates.

"We don't get many adoptions from local people," said B. Olson.

"We have a fair number of mustangs running on our ranch," Dad explained.

The redhead picked up on Dad's apologetic tone. "Have a look around," she invited, pointing out which corrals held mares, foals, and stallions. "And if you have any questions about the animals, just ask."

"Are they all *wild* horses?" Sam blurted.

Dad and the BLM woman looked puzzled.

"Yes, BLM is only charged with protecting free-roaming horses and burros." The redhead spoke slowly, as if she didn't want to mention Sam wasn't too smart.

Sam felt embarrassed, but she needed a plan before explaining her question.

At the risk of sounding even dumber, she asked another question. "What if a horse was free-roaming but not a mustang?"

"Like a domestic animal turned free?"

"Or one that escaped," Sam said.

The woman nodded, catching on. "We look for signs of domestication. Marks from the nose band of a halter, maybe." She sounded so proper, it surprised Sam when the woman rubbed the bridge of her own nose. "And we have a brand inspector with us when we capture horses. Branded animals are declared 'estray.' A second brand inspector checks horses before they're adopted, too, just to be sure."

Sam pretended to study a sorrel mare with white socks, but she was thinking, *The Phantom may not have a brand, but he's mine.*

"And if there isn't a brand?" Sam heard Dad's

boots shift as he listened.

"No lip tattoo or ear crop, either?" the woman asked, and Sam nodded. "The person claiming the animal might supply registration papers if the horse were a purebred—or convincing photographs."

Sam's spirits soared, then crashed. She had a photograph taken when her colt was eighteen months old, but she wouldn't call it convincing. In that picture, his coat was coal black.

"What about a scar?" Jake asked. Sam knew he'd remembered the mark from Slocum's rope. "Could someone get a horse back by explaining a scar?"

"Not a chance." The woman brushed away the suggestion as if it were a pesky fly. "Anyone could tell a story about a scar." She peered past the three of them toward the road, then turned to Dad. "You must be missing a horse."

"Not a one." Dad didn't give Sam a stern look, but she heard displeasure in his voice.

Miss Olson shrugged, then glanced toward an approaching cloud of dust. "That rumbling means it's time to return to work. This drought's caused us a couple of emergency gathers. If you'll excuse me."

Sam watched the woman go. Sam didn't trust her formality and she didn't like the way Miss Olson kept referring to horses as "animals." Even though they were.

As everyone turned to see the approaching vehicles, Sam noticed a cowboy who looked familiar. Not the bearded man she'd started thinking of as Bale Tosser, nor the clipboard man, but another man. His long, drooping mustache reminded her of someone, but she couldn't recall whom.

A huge truck labored up the road, but another truck, smaller than the other one and pulling a roomy gooseneck horse trailer, came first. Miss Olson started to walk away, then paused.

"The stallions are in the gooseneck," she said. "The mares are in the semi. You might enjoy watching us unload."

Dad glanced at Sam. She nodded, though something told her it wouldn't be fun.

The smaller truck backed the gooseneck trailer into position for a loading chute. Sam heard horses shifting, stamping, snorting. The stallions demanded release.

Men in cowboy hats checked the chute, tested gates, and unlocked latches. A few held long flexible whips with pieces of paper attached to the tips, probably to hurry the horses along. If they ever emerged.

Sam didn't know whether she longed for their appearance or dreaded it. Especially when she squinted at the horses jostling inside the trailer.

Like most horses, mustangs were usually bays and sorrels, but through the side of the trailer, Sam saw one creamy horse.

Miss Olson joined the man with the clipboard. They stood where they could see each horse appear.

It took forever for the trailer door to swing open. A neigh echoed. Hooves stumbled. More whinnies were followed by the snapping of teeth.

One horse slammed against the side of the trailer. When he tossed his head in distress, Sam saw it was the pale mustang.

Please not the Phantom, please.

Sam hadn't spoken aloud, but she realized her fingers were clenched in fists when Jake grabbed one of them. He unfolded her hand, gave it a squeeze, and held it, as the first stallion bolted out of the trailer and into the sunlight.

Chapter Ten ❧

𝒯HE FIRST STALLION was the color of orange sherbet mixed with whipped cream.

He was not the Phantom. Not even a gray. Sam sighed as if a metal band had been cut from around her chest.

The stallion had the thick neck of a mature horse, but he stood only a little taller than a pony. His long forelock swept back from his eyes as he charged into the empty corral. Then he trotted along the fence line, anxious for the company of other horses.

When he was joined by a leggy bay, taller but younger, they circled the pen together, forming a herd of two.

With all eight stallions penned, the truck full of mares began unloading into a larger corral.

The stallions seemed to ignore them, until the bay veered too close to the side of the pen nearest the mares. At once, the cream-colored stallion charged, reared, and came down to give the bay a savage bite on the crest.

Surprised and hurt, the bay fled to the opposite side of the corral. He stood trembling among the other stallions, while the pony-sized bully held his ground.

"It happens once in a while." Miss Olson stood next to them again. "But not often. Sometimes there's one horse just itching to prove he's in charge."

"Just like people," Jake said.

Sam thought of Slocum.

"Precisely," said the woman. Then she glanced at Sam. "We've got a vet who'll check that bite."

Sam held her breath. Miss Olson must have noticed Sam looked worried, but she couldn't know why—Sam was imagining a fight between the cream stallion and the Phantom. She had a feeling it wouldn't end so quickly or quietly.

The Phantom was used to surviving in the wild and fending for himself. In a place like this, challenged by other stallions, surrounded by fences and unfamiliar humans, he might believe he was fighting for his life.

Sam ducked her head a little, hoping to hide her eyes. It didn't matter, because Miss Olson's attention had moved on.

"Don't all those horses, loaded with potential, make you want to go on a shopping spree?" Miss Olson asked and Sam realized she was trying to sell Dad a horse.

"Not hardly," Dad said, but he looked amused.

"What about that black mare with white socks?" Miss Olson turned toward Sam and Jake. "Don't you kids think she'd be just right for your mom?"

Their voices overlapped, in response.

"He's not my dad," Jake corrected.

"My mom's dead," Sam said.

"I'm sorry," the woman said. She took a while to put together an explanation. "A man with two teenagers—" she began.

"Understandable," Dad said, but Sam thought he let the woman off the hook too quickly.

Sam couldn't believe Miss Olson didn't just slink off to her office. She didn't. She hadn't finished trying to find homes for the horses. Next, she sized up Jake.

"That buckskin filly is quick as a cat. I bet you could school her into a fine cutting horse."

Jake shook his head and the woman sighed.

"If I didn't have two mustangs and a wild burro already, I'd take her home with me."

Sam considered the woman's freshly pressed uniform and short, scrubbed fingernails. Sam couldn't imagine her working in a dirt corral with dust settling on her perfect French braid.

Dad squinted toward the corral, not the woman. When he nodded, Sam considered the horses again.

The buckskin had clean lines, a sloping shoulder for smooth gaits, and she wanted to belong. Separated from other mustangs, she might allow a human to substitute for her herd.

Grudgingly, Sam admitted to herself that Miss Olson had some horse sense. And she was trying to get these mustangs out of their pen and into real homes.

Sam scanned the newly arrived mares. If she were going to pick one for her own . . .

Then she caught herself. She had a horse. Besides, she didn't approve of the BLM. Wild horses should be running free.

Dad looked restless. Sam checked her watch and found they'd left home nearly two hours ago. Dad never spent this much time just hanging around.

"Best be going," Dad said. "Sam, Jake," he nodded toward the truck.

"Before you leave, I should introduce myself." The redhead extended her hand. "I'm Brynna Olson, director of the Willow Springs facility. Bring a horse trailer, next time you visit, Mr. —"

"Wyatt Forster," Dad said. As he shook the redhead's hand, Sam thought his tone was too friendly for a man who criticized the BLM so often.

Miss Olson leaned toward Sam. "Call me if you have more questions." Her voice dropped, as if the two of them might conspire against Dad. "Willow Springs is in the phone book under 'U.S. Government.'"

Back at the truck, Dad held the door so Sam could slide inside. As she climbed up, Sam saw Dad look back toward the corrals. Something told her he wasn't picking out a mustang.

"She only mentioned 'our mother' to find out if you were married." Sam couldn't believe the sneering voice was her own.

Still, she knew she was right. And even though Mom had been dead for eight years, she didn't like strangers bringing it up.

Dad's face turned crimson, and his expression looked more angry than embarrassed. Dad didn't speak to her, though; he just looked across the truck cab at Jake and said, "I'll drive."

Jake glared at Sam as if it were her fault he'd been demoted to the position of passenger. Once inside, he leaned against the door, as far from her as possible.

As they rattled along the road back to the ranch, Sam felt ashamed. If Brynna Olson *had* been flirting with her dad, why should she care?

Sam looked sideways at him. Dad's amused expression had turned into a frown. His hands gripped the steering wheel, hard, and his hat brim cast his face in shadow. He didn't look her way, even when Sam sucked in her breath as they drove through the narrow, dangerous pass Jake called Thread the Needle.

She glanced to her right. Jake wouldn't meet her eyes, either. He had one arm on the open window, and his face leaned into the wind.

As soon as the truck reached pavement and they picked up speed, Dad let her know he hadn't liked her remark.

"It wasn't a museum or a movie, but I thought you'd get a kick out of those horses," he said.

"I did."

She sure hadn't acted like it, his silence told her.

Sam knew she owed Dad an explanation. Just because she felt worried and confused over the Phantom, she didn't have to drag Dad down with her.

She thought of the quicksand. That afternoon, she'd acted like an adult. She'd given Dad a reason to be proud of her. It was time to do it again.

"Please pull over, Dad," she said. "We need to talk."

Sam told Dad and Jake everything. She listed each time the stallion had come to her and described the way he'd acted. She revealed everything except the hidden valley of wild horses and the Phantom's secret name. By the time Sam finished, even Dad suspected she was right.

"So you think it's Blackie," Dad said.

"It has to be."

"Jake, you've had a look." Dad stared passed Sam to Jake. "What do you think?"

Jake looked uneasy with the burden of Dad's trust.

"Couldn't say, based on the look I got. But if even

half of what Sam says is true, I'd bet my college fund on it."

"Are you exaggerating?" Dad asked.

Sam thought hard. "I can't read his mind or be sure he recognizes me, but he's come to the river twice. And I saw him two times on the cattle drive." She remembered the magical night ride with Ace and the Phantom racing side by side. "Once, he was almost close enough to touch."

"At the ranch and out there, it was the same horse," Dad said. "You're sure?"

"The same exact horse," Sam insisted. "Silver-white with gray dapples and a scar on his neck."

"I rarely see mustangs. Once in a while around the water hole, and then I run 'em off," Dad mused.

Sam felt startled, until she reminded herself that Dad might like wild horses, but he was a cattleman first. Every meal on the table and tank of gas in the truck depended on fat, healthy cattle. River Bend would die without them.

"If you've seen the same horse four times in a couple weeks," Dad continued, "that's just too often to be chance."

They all sat quietly. The smell of hot sage blew in the truck window. A meadow lark caroled liquid notes. A minivan from Vancouver rushed by and a crow jabbered as it hunted among weeds at the roadside.

"And there's not a darn thing we can do to get him back," Dad said.

"Not according to Miss Olson, but maybe some BLM hotshot could help," Jake suggested. "Do you know anyone, Wyatt?"

"Never had much use for the BLM," Dad said, then threw Sam a guilty look. "They're all just doing their jobs, but they make it tough to keep doing mine."

"I don't want him back," Sam blurted.

"What?" The word erupted from both Dad and Jake.

Sam had even surprised herself. She'd never thought it through, this far. But suddenly, Sam knew it was true.

"That's right," she said. "I don't want to tame him. I've got Ace to ride. I had a chance to make Blackie mine and I blew it. Now, he's learned to be free."

Sam smiled at Dad, too worried about sounding sappy to wonder why Jake's eyes closed as if she'd socked him in the stomach.

"You want him to stay on the range," Dad said.

"Unless Slocum—"

"Call him *Mr.* Slocum," Dad said. "Or *Linc* Slocum, at least."

Sam couldn't believe it. Just when she got to thinking how cool Dad was, he reverted to some code of the Old West. On this issue, she could not go along with him.

"Slocum doesn't deserve my respect," Sam insisted. Then, in spite of the confinement of the truck cab, she folded her arms.

Dad prepared to wait her out. His eyes stayed steady and Sam folded her arms even tighter.

Not for a second did she wonder which of them would win the stare-off. They might be equally stubborn, but she was *right*.

She would have outlasted Dad if Slocum's flashy tan Cadillac hadn't appeared just ahead. Honking a long blast, it swerved across the street's white center line and stopped beside Dad's truck.

Western music thumped from the car, even though the windows were closed. Then the driver's window slid down, releasing a blast of air-conditioning into the high desert heat.

Linc Slocum's slicked-back hair and toothpaste-commercial grin reminded Sam of the day she'd met him on her arrival home. This time he wore mirrored sunglasses and held a cigarette in one hand.

"Been up to Willow Springs?" He shouted over the music, instead of turning it down, and he didn't wait for an answer. "Find any range rats worth the drive?"

Range rats. Oh, sure. If that's what Slocum thought of wild horses, why had he spent two days chasing the Phantom?

Sam glanced out the truck's back window. Black asphalt stretched off to a heat-wavering horizon. They'd come a long way since they turned off the dirt road from Thread the Needle and the BLM corrals.

How could Slocum know where they'd been?

" 'Fraid we're coming home empty-handed," Dad said. "Just wanted to show Samantha what the government's built since she's been gone."

"There's nothing up there I want," Slocum said. "Even if they bring that white stud in—"

"Gray," Sam muttered to Jake.

"—I'm not sure I'd buy him. Although," Slocum took off his glasses and settled back in his seat, "there might be some Quarter blood in him. And maybe some Arab."

Sam felt a pang of surprise. Slocum was right. Blackie's sire, Smoke, had been a full-blooded mustang with the build of a Quarter horse. His mother Princess Kitty had been a racing Quarter horse, but she'd had the fine-boned head of an Arab. Somehow, she hadn't expected Slocum to know that much about horses.

Even though Smoke had been Dad's horse, even though he knew Slocum was right, Dad didn't encourage the man's speculation.

"Hard to say." Dad's response sounded like a dismissal, but as he started the truck's engine, Slocum kept talking.

"Not that I'd put him to my registered mares," Slocum mused.

Dad shifted uncomfortably.

"Still, he'd be good for breeding cow ponies. Those mustangs have good hard hooves, don't they?"

"Yeah," Dad said.

Why didn't Dad speak up and say there was more than hard feet to admire in a mustang? Why didn't he ask why Slocum needed cow ponies when he had more land and fewer cattle than any rancher in northern Nevada?

But even if Dad didn't want to chat, Slocum did.

"You heard what I'm doing, just before school starts?" Slocum rambled on, as if Dad had begged for details. "I'm getting both my kids new horses."

Sam made a mental note to ask Jake about Slocum's kids. How old were they, she wondered, and did they take after their dad?

"Yes sir," Slocum continued. "An Irish heavy hunter for Ryan and an English thoroughbred with blood lines from Queen Elizabeth's own stables for Rachel to use in dressage."

"That's great, Linc," Jake said. "But I thought Ryan was learning to rodeo."

"Not if his mother has anything to say about it. And, she does." Slocum frowned.

Did Slocum scowl because of the topic, or because he didn't like talking to Jake, a teenager who'd stood up to him?

Aunt Sue had always advised Sam to give people a chance. The better she got to know Slocum, though, the worse he got.

". . . keep that jug-headed range rat away from the real horses—" Slocum sneered.

"If 'jug-headed' means dumb, Mr. Slocum, I can't help thinking how much smarter a mustang would have to be." Sam kept her voice sweet, not mentioning how often the Phantom had outsmarted Slocum. "A mustang has to provide food, water, and shelter all for himself."

He was unprepared for the interruption. The way Dad's eyebrows shot up to disappear under his hat, so was he. But Sam had heard enough about range rats.

Sam took a breath, hoping her use of *mister* would keep Dad from punishing her.

"You'd think it would work that way, wouldn't you, little lady?" Slocum said. "But it just doesn't. Still, I could turn a good old-fashioned bronc buster loose on that Phantom. In an hour, he'd be thrown, hog-tied, sacked out, and taught some manners. Then I might make something of him."

Sam only understood half of what Slocum suggested, but she knew it was evil. He wanted to terrify her horse into obedience.

What she wanted was to dive headfirst out the driver's window and make Slocum shut up. But Dad moved to block her view of Slocum and Jake muttered, "Cool it," just loud enough for her to hear.

"You might have a good point, Samantha," Slocum said. "Dumb or not, those horses are tough. And cheap."

When Slocum pretended to contemplate their

combined wisdom, Sam felt sick. And Slocum's scheme only got worse.

"Since my wrangler, Flick, is working up at Willow Springs, trying to earn a few extra dollars, I'll have him watch for that stud."

Now she remembered the cowboy with the droopy mustache. On the cattle drive Flick had joked that even dudes with "good bloodlines" scared easily.

In the lull between two guitar-twanging tunes on the radio, Sam heard Slocum chuckle, and now she knew he was baiting her.

"Yep, that guarantees I'll be the first to know the stud's been captured, and the first to show the legendary Phantom who's boss."

Chapter Eleven ❧

$\mathcal{D}$AD REFUSED TO HEAD for home. He said Gram
wanted the entire day alone to work in her garden.
Dallas, as foreman, could see that the evening chores
were done.

Instead of cooking, Gram planned to build wire
cages to hold up gangly tomato plants. Instead of
washing clothes, she wanted to kneel in the dirt and
pull weeds, while the sun warmed her back. Most of
all, she wanted to hollow out basins around her
thirsty vegetables, so precious desert water could
wait in little pools before soaking slowly to the roots.

Sam understood and promised she wouldn't interfere with Gram's day off.

"I just want to check on Buddy," she told him. "I
won't get in Gram's way or ask for a single thing."

"Nope. I promised to keep us gone all day," Dad
said. "So, we'll stop at Clara's for dinner."

Clara's coffee shop looked like 1950s diners Sam

had seen in movies. It sat next to two houses and Phil's Fill-Up, a gas station that also stocked hardware and groceries. The settlement of Alkali had few citizens, but it was a friendly place and the only civilization between River Bend Ranch and Darton, where local kids went to school.

Inside, five tables crowded together and six round stools faced a counter. As Dad and Jake hung their Stetsons on a rack by the door, Sam read a faded banner stretched across one wall. It read HOME OF THE BEST PINEAPPLE UPSIDE-DOWN CAKE IN THE WORLD!

Dad ordered giant cheeseburgers and a mound of french fries. Sam ate quickly, but she waited for Dad to finish before asking more questions. When he folded his paper napkin, Sam pounced.

"How can we keep Mr. Slocum from getting my horse?" she asked.

"What makes you think he'll be caught?" Jake asked.

Sam refused to be sidetracked. She needed Dad's opinion.

"If he is caught," she asked, "what should we do?"

Dad sighed. "We'd have to adopt him, and that means money."

"I know, but Aunt Sue could send my birthday present early. You know she would, and she always gives me a hundred dollars."

Dad shook his head. Without his hat, he looked

exposed. He'd never accepted the embarrassment of Aunt Sue giving Sam so much money every year.

"That wouldn't pay the adoption costs, let alone his feed," Dad lowered his voice as the waitress brought the bill for lunch.

"I have my savings account," Sam began, but when Dad pointedly plopped his hand down on the bill, she closed her lips.

"I'll think about it, but if I'm going to be forking hay to an animal all winter long, he must be good for something. Handling cattle. Dragging in firewood. Riding out to check fence, even.

"On a ranch, we all earn our keep. You do chores, I see that the cattle operation turns a profit, and Gram does everything no one else has time for. Jake here"—Dad jerked a thumb in Jake's direction—"does as he's told."

"Yes, sir." Jake laughed.

But then Dad's smile faded. "I don't see a four-year-old stallion who's been running wild doing much but causing trouble."

Dad stood, dug in his pocket, then tossed some dollar bills on the table.

"You kids have some dessert and pay the bill. I'll be back after I see if Phil has a part I need for the well pump. That well needs to be redrilled," Dad said, almost to himself. "But until we can afford it, I'm going to patch it together for one more year."

Sam thought of San Francisco, where water

gushed every time you turned a handle. People complained about the cost each month when they paid bills, but the water never ran red with minerals and no one wondered if the supply would run dry.

Dad looked old and tired when he talked about money. When the restaurant door closed behind him, Sam sat looking at her folded hands.

"Just get me a candy bar," she told Jake as he walked toward the cash register.

A candy bar was half the price of pineapple upside-down cake, but did it matter if she saved Dad a dollar? *Let me think about it,* he'd said, but logic wouldn't solve this problem. She had to come up with something creative. Something no one else had considered possible.

Jake returned with two candy bars. Since the coffee shop was cool from the big-bladed fan overhead, and the only other person inside was the waitress eating her own lunch and reading a magazine, Sam and Jake stayed.

"Making that stallion useful would mean training him," Jake said.

"You're good at working with horses, Jake. I've been watching you with Pocahontas." Sam had watched Jake with the little pinto, and realized all over again how good he was with horses. "I know you could help me school him. You did it before."

Jake ignored the compliment. "It would mean gelding him, too."

Sam noticed the scuffs across Jake's knuckles as he unwrapped his candy slowly, giving his words time to sink in.

"But he would have such beautiful colts," she said.

Still, she knew he was right. Gelded horses were easier to train.

"I don't think Wyatt has much use for a breeding stallion around the place. They're unpredictable." Jake cleared his throat. "Besides, you've heard Slocum criticize mustangs, and what he says is mild. Lots of ranchers think they should be gunned down on sight."

Sam blocked the mental flash of a rifle shot and horses falling.

"You're saying no one would pay to breed mares to him," Sam said. "No matter how strong, fast, and smart he is?"

"I know it sounds harsh, but it's true."

"Besides, he'd be miserable," Sam said.

"*Dangerous*, Sam. When that stallion is scared, he's dangerous. Got it?"

"Yes, I've got it."

Sam glanced over to see if the waitress had looked up from her magazine at the sound of their bickering. She hadn't.

"You might be right," Sam admitted. "Think of that little stallion staking out his territory in the Willow Springs corral."

"I didn't say a stallion like him, Sam. I said, that particular stallion. The Phantom. Blackie. Whatever you called him before. He nearly killed you."

This time, Jake's guilt didn't turn him pale. His ruddy skin grew darker.

"He wasn't trying to —"

"Sam. Shut up." Jake grabbed Sam's wrist before she could push back her chair and stomp out of the restaurant. "Sorry. I didn't mean 'shut up.' Could you just listen a minute? This talk between us has been a long time coming. We're going to have it now."

Sam's hands shook when Jake took his away.

"Most of the time, I don't think we should even hang around together." Jake looked at her from the corner of his eye, like a nervous horse. "I can't help teasing you, and you take it as a dare. That's why you keep getting in trouble."

"I get in trouble on my own," Sam said. "You've got nothing to do with it."

"Don't try to lead me off the subject, Sam. We're going to talk about that day."

Jake was right. She did *not* want to relive that day. In her lap, Sam's hands curled into fist and her fingernails bit into her palms.

"When I tried all that Native American horse taming stuff with Blackie —"

"It worked," she interrupted, then put her fingers over her lips. "Sorry, I'll be quiet now. But it *did* work."

"Yeah. Most of it I'd do over again. Some stuff I still do with rough stock your dad turns over to me. When you gave him a secret name, sighed your breath into his nostrils, and mounted him for the first time in the river, it all worked."

Jake's eyes grew dreamy as he remembered. "That colt was yours, body and soul."

Jake looked up then, sharply. "But he's still got a horse's brain. We couldn't trust him to think for himself."

"It was my idea to leave the ranch grounds," Sam said, remembering the second day she'd ridden Blackie.

"I was older. I knew better."

"I remember begging," Sam said.

"So what? I shouldn't have given in to a little kid."

The wind had come up outside the restaurant. Dust pecked at the window. There were no trees and few other buildings to slow its force.

It had been a windy day at River Bend, when she'd sweet-talked Jake into letting her ride Blackie.

He'd agreed, but only if she met his list of requirements. Jake told her to ride bareback, so she did. He insisted something soft be used for Blackie's first bitless bridle, so Sam fashioned an outgrown red flannel nightgown into a headstall and attached cotton rope reins.

As they'd set out, the colt looked flashy and responded like a dream. He'd welcomed Sam's small weight on his back and her hand resting on his withers. His wide eyes took in everything and his slim black legs pranced as they'd passed the ranch house, angled through pastures, and headed for the open range.

"Everything was going fine," Jake's voice narrated the pictures in Sam's mind. "You followed my directions, exactly."

"Because I looked up to you, Jake, even though you called me a brat and a tagalong and teased me unmercifully." Sam was joking, but Jake's downcast expression said she'd made him feel even worse.

"I only planned to take you out a mile or so, but Blackie was doing so great, we just kept riding."

"It showed how much time we'd taken gentling him," Sam added. "You taught me a lot, Jake."

Jake didn't seem to hear her.

"All the way out, I opened the gates and closed them behind us. I don't know why I thought that was such a chore."

From her earliest days, Sam had known that major ranch rule. If a rider came to a gate that was open, the gate was left open. If it was shut, the rider had to ride through, then back his horse and close it.

"Coming back, I let you ride ahead, so you could maneuver Blackie to open the gate. You'd only been riding him for one day, though, and it was windy. Blackie was already starting to spook at blowing sagebrush. What was I thinking making you fight those gates?"

Sam thought she'd forgotten most of that day, but details came back with the remembered scent of dust on summer wind and Jake's shout.

"Ride in parallel to the gate," Jake had yelled. "Parallel, brat. Get him to face the hinge. That's it. Now rattle the gate. Whoa, keep him together. Now ride back and do it again. Parallel. Rattle it. See? He's not as scared this time."

Blackie had tensed beneath her. She'd felt his sweat soak through her jeans. But he'd trusted her. By the third time Sam rattled the gate, the colt didn't tremble.

But holding the gate open and getting the horse through wasn't easy. By then, Sam was sweating, too.

"Pull the gate towards you. Don't take your hand off it."

"Jake, it's too hard. He's scared."

Sam could still hear her quavering voice, and she'd known her hands, shaking on the reins, only made the colt more afraid.

"Just back him through, or turn him," Jake's impatience made Sam feel clumsy. "Don't take your hand off the gate, I said. Sam, get a grip."

The black colt had danced in place, tossing his head. His black mane stung her cheeks and her arm ached from holding the gate open. Her legs quivered from urging the horse to obey.

"Jake, he's really scared," she said over Blackie's snorts. "You have to get this gate. I can't."

All right, you baby. The words echoed in Sam's mind. Had he really said them? Sam looked at Jake across the table and asked.

"Yeah, I said it," Jake admitted. "And soon as you twisted around in your saddle to start yelling that you'd slug me if I didn't take it back, Blackie fell apart. He charged into the gate. You lost your hold on it and Blackie thought he was trapped.

"His shoulders were only pinned for a minute, but he reared to escape. I tried to ride in and help, but he bolted backward, slamming into my horse. You stayed on, until he took off for open range."

That's when she'd lost her reins. Sam remembered leaning against the colt's neck, looking down at the gray-green desert floor speeding by in a blur as the ropes swirled around the colt's running legs.

Why hadn't she just held tight and ridden out his fear? Why had she stretched, reaching down to grab them? It made no sense to her now, but she had.

"And when you leaned down on the left to grab your reins, he caught a glimpse of you and veered hard right. You went one way, he went the other, and his off hind hoof caught you in the head."

Like a drumbeat she'd never forget, Sam heard those hooves pounding away. She felt weak, as if she'd lived it all over again. As if she were lying shaken on the ground.

"I don't remember much after that," she said.

"You were unconscious. Your head was bleeding.

I knew head wounds bled a lot. I knew it, but it was *your* head. And there was so much . . . blood." Jake separated the last two words with silence. "I didn't know what to do."

What *should* he have done? Sam didn't know, and yet she was thirteen now, the same age Jake had been then.

Water rushed against a metal sink as someone washed dishes in the restaurant kitchen. The waitress closed her magazine, stretched, and carried her plate across the room on squeaky tennis shoes.

"Can I get you two something else?" she asked.

"No, we're just going," Jake said.

What should he have done? Sam swept the candy wrappers into a pile. Then she and Jack stood and headed for the door. Jake took his black Stetson from the rack, as she threw the wrappers away.

Sam squinted against blowing dust as they left Clara's and walked toward Phil's Fill-Up.

"It was the hardest thing I've ever done, galloping away, leaving you there all alone."

Sam tried to catch Jake's arm. She wanted to tell him that he couldn't help being a dumb kid, that he had no right to keep shouldering this guilt.

She felt Jake's bicep tense as he shook free of her hand, refusing comfort. He kept striding toward the gas station and Sam rushed to keep up.

"I'd heard not to move folks who were badly injured, so I didn't. But the whole way back to River

Bend, and the entire trip riding out, leading your dad to you, I kept promising God that if you weren't dead, I'd watch over you better."

Sam bit the inside of her cheek. She certainly didn't want to interfere with Jake's bargain, but she didn't want a constant watchdog either.

"And I wasn't dead. Which is great." Sam made her voice cheerful. "But I'm a big girl now and I can take care of myself."

Jake stopped. He faced her in the middle of the sidewalk.

"A promise is a promise, Sam. Get used to it. I won't let anyone, including Wyatt, give that horse a second chance to kill you."

Chapter Twelve ❧

IT TOOK SAM MORE than a few steps to shake off Jake's announcement.

They had almost reached the truck when she saw Dad hold up a small cardboard box. The pump part must be inside, because he looked pretty happy.

When Jake gave Dad a smiling thumbs-up, the tension waned and Sam finally asked the question that had nibbled at her all afternoon.

"If Buddy were crying for her lunch from the pasture and Gram was in the garden, she'd hear, wouldn't she?"

"I don't know," Jake said. "Which pasture? Did you put her out with the horses?"

"No, the other pasture."

"Right by the barn?" Jake shook his head. "If you got those rails back up, alone, you're stronger than you look, Wonder Woman."

"Rails?" Sam's stomach sank.

"The fence rails. We lowered them to back the truck in with hay last week. I should've had them back up by now, but since we weren't using it . . ." Jake's words trailed off as he watched her.

"I hope Buddy didn't find the opening in the fence."

"She couldn't have missed it, Sam. How could you not see the rails laying in the grass? They opened a hole big enough to drive a truck through."

"I was in a hurry this morning." Sam's lips felt numb as she mumbled the words.

On the ride home, neither Sam nor Jake mentioned her mistake. Jake had changed a lot. Two years ago, he would have rushed to Wyatt to announce her blunder.

Hurry, hurry. It can't be too late. Oh please, let it not be too late. Sam leaned forward in her seat, as if she could make the truck move faster.

As late afternoon grayed into dusk, Dad offered to drop Jake at home. Jake said he'd ride Witch from River Bend.

"Suit yourself," Dad said. "But it's coming on dark."

By the time the truck rumbled over River Bend bridge, the sky had turned ink-blue. Only the bottoms of clouds were orange from the setting sun.

When the truck headlights showed Gram, dressed for riding and leading Ace, Sam's dread turned to fear. Had she saved Buddy's life just to lose her now?

She glanced at Jake. So, this was how it felt to be guilty and totally to blame.

"What is it?" Dad called out the window, before he stopped the truck.

"The calf's disappeared. I didn't go in for lunch until quite late. Then, I noticed her bottle in the refrigerator. I'd forgotten all about it," Gram said. "I was surprised she hadn't reminded me with her bawling. I've scouted all over on foot and I was just getting ready to ride out, calling for her."

"Let me go." Sam was out of the truck, reaching for Ace's reins. "Please."

"In a minute," Dad said. "First explain how this happened."

Sam knew she had no choice.

"This morning, before I knew we were going to Willow Springs, I turned Buddy out into the pasture."

"Which pasture?"

Sam glanced at Jake. "The one with the rails down."

"Did you put them back up?" Dad looked at Jake as if he might have helped.

"No. I, uh, didn't notice they were down," Sam admitted. "About an hour ago, I mentioned what I'd done, to Jake, and he told me the rails had been down for a week."

Sam felt herself shrink as Dad stared at her.

"Better get going," he said, finally. He shooed her with one hand, as if he wanted her out of his sight.

"I'll get Witch and ride along," Jake said.

"No, you won't," Dad barked. "That calf was Sam's responsibility, Jake. Let her go."

Sam didn't know where to start, but she didn't ask for help. Instead, she tried to think like a cow. She started at the downed rails and rode through every gate that stood ajar, zigzagging on a path that led toward open range.

The afternoon's breeze had turned into a cold night wind, but Sam wouldn't turn back for a jacket.

Buddy could be lost. Her soft fur could be snagged on barbed wire. Those delicate legs could be trapped between rocks in a ravine.

The calf was a baby, too young to be out alone. Whatever happened to her, Sam would be to blame.

When Sam heard a quick series of yips, she stopped Ace. She watched the gelding's ears. They swivelled forward, locating the coyotes, but he didn't turn skittish, so Sam rode on.

Dark clouds blew across the moon's surface, dimming light that might have helped her search. Sam stopped, and stared into the near-darkness. Dad must be terribly angry to let her come out in the dark, alone, where anything could happen.

Ace heard Buddy first. The gelding froze, head

level and ears pricked forward.

Sam heard the calf bawl, but then the sound cut off. Why?

With nightmarish uncertainty, Sam rode another step. Stopped. Rode a step. Turned her head to listen. She couldn't give up, but she couldn't tell where Buddy's cry had come from, either. Finally, she trusted Ace.

"You're the one with the cow sense. I'm just a tenderfoot." Sam rubbed the mustang's neck. "See if you can find her, please?"

She gave Ace his lead and he stepped out with confidence. Soon, he trotted through the darkness, jumpy but unafraid.

Two coyotes had Buddy cornered. With her tail flat against a fence post and her head lowered for a charge, the calf did her best to protect herself.

It wasn't good enough.

One coyote rushed in to nip the calf's flank. When Buddy faced her attacker, the other coyote darted for her shoulder.

"No!" Sam shouted. She clapped her heels against Ace's sides and sent him running forward.

The gelding liked nothing about this. Not the calf bawling toward the sky. Not the coyotes, who'd paired up and backed off a few yards. The gelding slowed into a shambling gait, but he didn't refuse to run between the calf and the coyotes.

When Buddy saw yet another monster, Ace,

bearing down on her, she sprinted past.

The coyotes followed the calf.

"Stop it! Go on, get away!" Still holding her reins, Sam slid from Ace's saddle. She picked up a rock and heaved it.

The coyotes dodged, then stood watching her. Moonbeams broke through the clouds, spotlighting them for a moment. Absolutely doglike, the coyotes stood watching, heads tilted, confused by Sam's screaming.

"Get out of here!" Sam's voice rasped this time.

She was breathless and scared, and the coyotes knew it. They trotted only a few steps before looking back. Sam tried to take a deep breath, but it hurt. The coyotes probably thought they could take Buddy away from her. And they were right.

Desperate, Sam held her arms out wide, flapped them, and rushed forward.

Apparently, the coyotes didn't want to try their luck against a crazy person. They broke into an easy lope and didn't even break stride as they ducked under a fence. Before Sam's eyes, they disappeared on the sage-spotted plain.

At last, Buddy recognized her. The calf meandered closer, snuffling, then leaned against Sam's legs. All she had to do was get the calf up across Ace's saddle, and it would be a short ride home. Dad would be proud of her. Or at least not quite so angry.

And she'd do it. In a minute.

With one hand, Sam rubbed Buddy's ears. With the other, she held her reins, so she couldn't cover her mouth when she yawned.

"You don't care, do you, Ace?" Her words came out in a muffled roar and suddenly, Ace was done cooperating.

He backed to the end of the reins. His ears tilted out, until he looked like a mule. When she lifted Buddy and staggered forward, Ace continued backing, shaking his head.

"C'mon, Ace," she puffed, but the gelding refused to stand.

When Sam tripped and fell on top of the exhausted calf, Ace snorted and pawed the ground.

Sam struggled back to her feet and faced the horse. She shouldn't give in to him. If she did, he'd learn misbehaving got him what he wanted. But Sam was too tired to fight.

She wanted to be home, warming the backs of her legs in front of the fireplace, before she crawled into bed.

"Okay, you win." Sam took the rope from her saddle, settled a loop gently around Buddy's neck and led her home.

Buddy's bottle was in the barn, waiting. Once she had suckled and fallen asleep, Sam brushed Ace and turned him loose in the pasture. Then she got furious all over again at the coyotes.

The awful animals had been laughing at her, but

they hadn't been playing with Buddy. Although she'd examined the calf and found she wasn't bleeding, Sam knew they would have kept up their in-and-out assaults until the confused calf gave up. Then they would have launched the final attack.

Sam stamped her boots on the wooden porch and flung open the kitchen door so hard it hit the wall.

Dad and Gram turned away from the stove.

"I hate coyotes." Sam swallowed the quaver in her voice. "They tried to eat Buddy."

Sam didn't get the sympathy she expected.

"And whose fault is that?" Dad passed Sam a cup of hot cocoa and stood watching her.

"What do you mean?" Sam croaked, but she knew exactly what he meant.

"It's a coyote's job to feed her young and herself. Mostly she does that by killing old animals and weak ones." Dad's lecturing tone said he expected a response.

"I know," she said.

"I don't like losing cattle to coyotes, but some calves are orphaned and they become prey. The herd moves on, too fast for them to keep up and they starve, all alone. That makes a coyote kill almost merciful, don't you think?"

Dad waited for Sam to nod.

"Mother Coyote doesn't figure on human interference. She didn't know this little one was yours. She never would have laid eyes on it, if you"—Dad stared at Sam—"hadn't neglected that calf. So don't go blaming the coyotes."

Dad left. She heard him collapse into a recliner in the living room. Then came the drone of television news.

Sam couldn't work up the energy to feel sorry for herself, or to pull out a chair and sit. She covered her face with her chilled hands, until Gram guided her to the table.

Gram placed a grilled cheese sandwich and a green teapot full of cocoa on the table before her.

Never in all her thirteen years had Sam heard her father string so many words together. Dad had chosen every one to prove she was irresponsible. And a disappointment.

If she added together all that had happened today, she should be too miserable to eat.

Sam closed her eyes and saw the horse fight at Willow Springs. Once more, she heard Slocum's leering promise to get his hands on the Phantom. And she felt the helpless guilt of knowing she'd put Buddy in danger.

All the same, Sam was famished. She took a bite of the buttery, toasted sandwich, then sat back, chewing.

"Gram?"

Gram pulled up a chair and sat down. Breaking all her own rules, Gram put both elbows on the table and held her chin.

"Yes, Sam."

"Do you think I'll be grounded until I'm nineteen?"

"No, dear. I think your father was just shocked you'd do something so careless."

"I thought you were on my side," Sam mumbled.

"You know very well this isn't about sides. Next time, your carelessness might hurt you."

Sam wondered if the clock had stopped. It must be later than eight o'clock.

"You'll never know how hard it was for him," Gram took a shuddering breath. "For both of us, when you got hurt. For days, we waited to see if you'd be able to walk or talk again. He doesn't want it to happen ever again."

"Then why did he let me go out there—" Sam waved a hand toward the range. "Gram, it was creepy being out there all alone."

"I'm sure you didn't like it, but if you touched your dad's coat, hanging on the back of the kitchen door," Gram said, "you'd feel it's still cold. You were never alone, Sam."

Sam sagged against the chairback. Her body wanted sleep, but her mind kept chattering.

Gram reached across to pat Sam's hand.

"Your father's a pretty level-headed man. I think he'll get over it."

Gram had hardly finished speaking when Dad stormed back into the kitchen.

"And another thing," he began. "If you aren't

mature enough to handle a six-week-old calf, what will you do with a mustang stallion?" Dad paced between the table and the refrigerator, then pointed his index finger at her. "The adoption is no longer open for discussion!"

This time, when he left the room, Dad clomped upstairs.

Gram and Sam exchanged shocked expressions. They both heard the echo of Gram saying Dad would soon "get over" Sam's mistake.

"Then again," Gram said, looking up as something—maybe a boot—hit Dad's bedroom wall upstairs, "I might be wrong."

Chapter Thirteen ⬿

 $\mathcal{L}$ AY LOW.

After her near-disaster with Buddy, Sam could think of no other way to avoid her father's anger.

For three days she did chores and kept her room neat. Without being asked she helped Gram in the kitchen and vegetable garden. She folded laundry.

At night Sam studied the mustang adoption application. If Slocum made one move toward adopting the Phantom, she'd try to stop him. Sam paid special attention to the section listing "prohibited acts." If half of what she'd heard about Slocum was true, he was in big trouble.

Sam was a good student, and two weeks without classes made this kind of work exciting, even fun. She filled pages of the purple stationary Aunt Sue had given her with reasons Linc Slocum might be ineligible to adopt. She couldn't wait to pass her research on to Miss Olson.

The opportunity probably wouldn't come soon, because Dad hadn't finished punishing her.

Yesterday when Dad told her to scrub out the watering trough, she'd done it. The backbreaking chore left her arms trembling, but she didn't answer back when Dad took one look and sent her back to do it right.

Sam spent two more hours scouring the metal. When she finished, it looked like Dad had bought it the day before. She didn't expect any praise for her accomplishment and she didn't get any. Still, Dad couldn't conceal his surprise at how good it looked during his final inspection.

Now that Sam had changed the straw in Buddy's stall, she laid down the pitchfork. Standing in the barn door, she glanced around. Everyone was busy outdoors, so Sam sneaked toward the house.

What she was about to do wasn't wrong, but Dad might not like it. She wished she could ask Jake if he thought Dad would be mad if he discovered she'd called the Willow Springs Wild Horse Center.

But Jake wasn't around. Sam hadn't asked why or where, but her imagination had supplied lots of answers. Though Jake hadn't caused her to put Buddy in the wrong pasture, maybe Dad thought he'd distracted her. Or Dad might have decided to save money by firing him.

She didn't think he would fire Jake, but she hadn't thought Dad could ever be so angry, either.

As she crossed the yard, Sam glanced toward the river. It was a reflex triggered by the fact that she hadn't seen her silver stallion for four nights. Could the stallion know she'd made a big mistake and didn't deserve his company?

Still, he deserved her protection and she'd give it to him, even if it meant defying Dad.

Inside, Sam heard only the refrigerator's purr and the ticking of the kitchen clock. Two o'clock. Good timing, since the BLM office closed at four.

She'd dialed the number twice before. Each time, Sam had to erase her nerves with a pep talk and a reminder that Miss Olson had encouraged her to call.

The first time, Sam had called anonymously. She'd asked if any new horses had been rounded up. A voice she recognized as Miss Olson's described the herd Sam had seen. Reassured that the Phantom was still free, Sam had hung up, satisfied.

Yesterday, when she still hadn't seen the stallion, Sam had called again. Miss Olson's answer was the same: no new horses.

It was getting easier to call, but this morning, she'd begun worrying over Flick. She knew he'd call Slocum the instant the Phantom was unloaded. Sam couldn't take any chances.

She hadn't figured out what she'd do if Miss Olson said, "Yes, as a matter of fact, we just brought in a splendid silvery gray stallion."

Sam just had to know.

She dialed and asked the usual question.

Instead of the usual answer, Miss Olson asked a question in return. "May I ask who's calling?"

Sam's hand gripped the telephone receiver and she blurted the truth. "This is Samantha Forster."

"Hi Samantha, this is Brynna Olson. We met the other day." She sounded as if she'd known the truth all along.

Sam glanced out the kitchen window. No one was headed this way. "Oh, hi," she said, as casually as she could.

"You know, we don't do much gathering this time of year," Miss Olson said. "February through July are quiet months, unless there's a problem horse or an emergency gather, like the one the other day. We try to hold off until August, so we don't stress the spring foals."

"That's good," Sam said. She was surprised by the BLM's humanity. This also meant she had time to pass on what she had learned about Slocum.

"Samantha, is there a particular horse you're waiting for? Because if there is—"

"No ma'am, of course not." Sam looked out the window in time to see Gram stand and peel off her gardening gloves. "I've got to go now." Gram began walking toward the house. "Thanks for the information."

"But Samantha—"

"Bye." Sam hung up, grabbed a glass, and jerked

the ice tray from the refrigerator just as Gram came inside.

"Ice water?" Sam asked.

She hoped Gram couldn't hear her pounding heart. Probably not, since Gram only washed her hands and asked if Sam would help make a sauce for the spareribs they'd barbecue for dinner.

When a white BLM truck rumbled over the bridge to River Bend at five o'clock, it was a complete surprise to everyone except Sam.

Work had ended earlier than it had to today, because Gram, for the first time in Sam's memory, had made a miscalculation. Only after everyone quit chores to come in and clean up before dinner did Gram discover the barbecue fire had fizzled before the spareribs were cooked.

Since Pepper, Ross, and Dallas were already eating in their bunkhouse kitchen, and Sam and Dad had showered, there was no sense returning to work. So, Gram turned her mistake festive. She restarted the coals, then served tortilla chips, salsa, and lemonade on the front porch while they waited for the ribs to cook.

Before gobbling her own snack, Sam walked down to the ten-acre pasture to give Ace an apple. The little mustang had never been pampered, and he was beginning to like it.

That's where she was when Miss Olson arrived.

Glancing over her shoulder, Sam saw Dad stand and shade his eyes. Her only hope was to get to Miss Olson before he did.

"Hi," the redhead said as she slammed the truck door behind her. "Since you're interested, I thought I'd drop by and do an informal preadoption inspection."

Informal or not, the word *inspection* sounded official. Dad wouldn't like it a bit.

With the apple still clutched in her hand, Sam rushed forward. "I can't, you know, make any deals behind my dad's back," she whispered.

Miss Olson surprised her by laughing. Once more, Sam noticed the sun lines around her blue eyes.

"Even if you could hide a horse, you'd have to be eighteen to adopt." Brynna followed Sam's worried peek toward the porch.

"He doesn't miss much," Sam admitted. "And he's dead set against adopting a mustang."

"What about your pal, there?" Brynna nodded toward Ace.

Sam saw the little bay had followed her. He stretched his neck over the fence, showing the freeze mark beneath his mane. He extended his head and fluttered his lips, begging for the apple.

"That's Ace."

"He's one of ours, though, right?"

"No." Sam's anger flared. "Ace is mine."

Miss Olson was quiet long enough to retuck her

uniform shirt into her khaki pants. Sam felt embarrassed. Just the same, Sam would not apologize to a woman who worked for an agency that not only leeched away Dad's money with high grazing fees, but could end the Phantom's freedom in an afternoon.

"I meant, he's a mustang the BLM brought in from the range." Miss Olson turned her head, moving her lips as if she were reading the white hairs in Ace's freeze mark. "Clearly, since he's been captive for two and a half years, he belongs to your family."

Sam's curiosity nearly got the better of her, but she would not ask how to read the mishmash of angles that composed the freeze mark.

"Who gentled him? You?" Miss Olson watched Ace grab the apple in one chomp.

"No, not me. I don't know who did," Sam said.

She knew it had been Jake, but the less this woman knew, the better.

Ace nodded as if he agreed, so Sam didn't mention he was a prime cutting horse, too.

Up and down went Ace's Arab-shaped head, and he drooled as he enjoyed the apple.

"Most of them make the transition quite well, if people take the time to understand it's hard shifting from freedom to captivity."

"If you know that, why do you trap them? Those helicopters, trucks, and pens must cost thousands of dollars—"

"Millions, actually." Miss Olson folded her arms

along the top rail to watch the other horses.

"So why do you do it?" Sam found the woman's composure obnoxious. "Just to make them miserable?"

Finally, the redhead stood back and met Sam's eyes.

"Number one, they'd die of dehydration. The range has too little water for ranchers' cattle and native wildlife, let alone horses with no natural predators.

"Number two," she drew a breath and ticked off a finger for another argument, "they'd starve, because of the competition for graze.

"Number three—and this isn't nice, but you look like a girl who appreciates the truth—the BLM is charged with *protecting* free-roaming horses from folks who want them dead."

Brynna Olson's argument had been so passionate, Sam almost didn't hear her father's boots crunch the gravel on the driveway.

As Sam watched him approach, she felt the tension of the argument drain away. She was pretty sure he'd drive Brynna Olsen off his land.

"You ladies having a squabble?" Dad asked.

Oh no, Sam thought. Would this get her into more trouble?

"More of a political discussion," said Miss Olson.

Dad's prickly attitude stayed focused on Miss Olson. "So, did we pass?"

"This wasn't," Miss Olson's voice faltered, "I mean, since you haven't applied for adoption . . ."

Any minute, Miss Olson might give away their secret conversations.

"But if it was an official inspection, would we pass?" Dad asked.

"Looks like it," Miss Olson's poise returned as she looked at the ranch with a professional eye. "Your facilities are adequate. Sufficient exercise space, shelter, good drainage. Is that fence six feet tall?" She pointed toward the round pen where Jake worked young horses.

"Yep."

Brynna smiled as Ace nibbled the collar of Sam's fresh blue tee shirt. "You'd probably pass, *if* you decided to apply."

Sam thought of the folded sheets of purple paper in her room. This was a perfect opportunity to tell what she knew, but she felt sheepish. Sam considered Miss Olson's pressed uniform and the sharp way she'd rattled off the reasons mustangs were gathered. Would Miss Olson think Sam was trying to tell her how to do her job?

Before Sam could puzzle out the possibilities, Gram's voice carried from the porch.

"Wyatt?"

Sam could tell Gram was reminding Dad of something.

Dad looked awkward as he asked, "Miss Olson,

would you like to stay for dinner?"

Sam almost chuckled. That *had* to be Gram's idea. Dad would never invite a BLM employee to sit at their table.

"I didn't mean to interrupt your meal," Miss Olson said.

"You didn't. Our barbecue fire fizzled." Sam stopped talking when she met her dad's eyes.

Miss Olson looked at her watch. "I couldn't, really."

Dad didn't press her, only shook hands and thanked her for stopping by before leaving Sam to walk Brynna back to her truck.

Looking at the woman's neat braid, Sam wished again that she hadn't cut her long hair. Sam had hacked it off so she wouldn't look like the kid who'd left River Bend ranch. How childish was that?

But she was done acting like a kid. It was time to ask Miss Olson for hard facts.

"What kind of emergency made you round up that last herd?"

The woman wet her lips in confusion, then remembered this afternoon's conversation. "Dust pneumonia," she answered. "The herd was in a severe drought area."

Sam thought of the wild horse valley, knee-deep in grass. The Phantom was safe there, but he ranged over a wide area, as he'd shown her by coming to River Bend.

Miss Olson climbed into the truck and slammed the door. She just sat for a minute, and Sam saw the woman was unwilling to leave things in such a tangle.

"I don't know what's going on with you, Samantha, but I might be able to help, if you would tell me what has you so worried."

Sam bit her lip. BLM was the enemy, but Brynna seemed genuinely concerned. Should she believe what Dad had told her, or the evidence in front of her? Sam wished she knew what to do.

So far, this entire summer had presented her with one decision after another, and her choices hadn't all turned out so great.

Then Brynna seemed to go veering off on a wild tangent.

"I have three horses," the woman said, abruptly. "And you know which one works with me like magic, like we were one animal instead of two? Penny, my little blind mustang."

"I can't imagine anything scarier than galloping into the darkness, because the stranger on your back told you to do it," Sam said.

Brynna pointed at Sam, as if she'd gotten an answer right in class. "Penny does it because she trusts me."

The truck's gears made a grinding sound. Brynna backed the truck a couple of feet before she added, "Sometimes blind trust can be the most perceptive of all."

Chapter Fourteen ∽

SAM SWUNG HER sleeping bag over one shoulder.

On this moonless night, she had only starshine to show the way along the gravel driveway, past the pasture and down to the river's edge.

Things grew quiet behind her. She heard the soft crunch of her tennis shoes, a whicker as Ace, alone as usual, followed along the fence line, and the occasional hoot of an owl.

Since luck was sitting on her shoulder tonight, Sam had decided to test Brynna Olson's blind-trust theory.

After their picnic supper of spareribs, garlic bread, and salad, the family had enjoyed a long talk. No one mentioned her mistake with Buddy, but Dad seemed ready to believe she'd learned her lesson.

Crickets hushed as Sam picked up rocks and plopped them into the river. She smoothed her sleeping bag on the ground she'd cleared, but she didn't try to sleep. She sat, tugged the cuffs of her gray sweatpants to cover her ankles, and pushed only her bare feet into the sleeping bag's cozy layers. Then she gazed into the high desert sky.

Blind trust. She wasn't sure what Brynna meant by it, and was less sure the stallion could feel such faith in her.

As a foal, he had, but that was a long time ago. Too many scary times had cropped up since then. Most of them involved people.

She'd been the one astride the young horse as he was held trapped by the gate. Later, a man had nearly strangled him with a rope and weight. Since then, helicopters had pursued him and he'd been run hard and long by Slocum and his Thoroughbred.

Zanzibar was a wild thing now. He couldn't trust her as a tame horse trusted its master. He might trust her as a friend.

Sam stared into the darkness, silently calling the stallion. The river ran murmuring by, but she heard nothing else.

For a long, cold time, she stared across the river, glad she'd left her watch inside. She shrugged her shoulders and wiggled her toes, keeping her muscles moving. When she finally burrowed into her sleeping bag, with only her face exposed to the night air, she still wouldn't allow herself to sleep.

And so Sam sang.

Ears pricked to catch each word, the horses lined

the pasture fence. Sam thought her voice sounded pretty good, pure and almost pretty, as it rose into the black and diamond sky.

Sam had run out of songs with memorable lyrics, when she thought of Christmas carols. Even on the last night of June, "Silent Night" sounded great.

The stallion appeared on the opposite bank, hazy as a chalk outline left after erasing a blackboard. Head raised on his graceful neck, he listened.

With a powerful plunge, the stallion rushed into the water, coming toward her, mane billowing on wind created by his own speed.

Spellbound, Sam stopped singing. Then she scolded herself. Last time, she'd frightened him with silence. For some reason, the stallion expected sound from her, so Sam kept singing.

Slowly, she slipped out of her sleeping bag, stood and walked to meet him.

The stallion slowed his swimming.

Did he remember she'd first ridden him in the river? Far back in his equine memory, did the stallion feel the soft flannel halter?

Did he hear echoes of Sam's whispers as she'd grabbed his mane and vaulted softly upon his back?

"All is calm . . ." Sam sang. She was in the river now and amazed that the water warmed her legs. Underfoot, the stones felt smooth. "All is bright . . ."

As she walked, Sam trailed her fingers in the river. It felt thicker than water. The closer she got, the more certain Sam grew that she could touch the stallion.

Once, he lowered his head and skimmed his muzzle along the river. Water splashed as if he meant to play.

"Zanzibar," she crooned, and lifted her right hand from the river.

He bolted.

For one heart-stopping second Sam thought she'd seen the last of him. At least for tonight. Instead, he scampered like a puppy, moving three watery lunges upstream, before prancing back to her, pushing waves before him that crashed over Sam's legs.

"Good horse, Zanzibar."

He stood two horse lengths away. Heat from his silver body made mist that clouded his form in the darkness.

"That's my boy," Sam said, slowly moving toward him.

His head snapped sideways, looking toward the ridge marking the boundary between River Bend and Slocum's ranch. Light flared like a low-hanging shooting star, and the horse trembled before looking back to her.

"Zanzibar," she said to him again, stopping. She kept her hand outstretched, but still.

If the stallion lowered his head now, his muzzle would touch her hand. His nostrils distended to study her scent.

Sam knew why. The stallion had seen her in many forms. Sometimes she approached him on Ace, so she'd seem to have horse's legs. He'd seen her working in the barnyard, afoot. And tonight, she must seem legless, flowing toward him like a mermaid.

Only scent promised it was her.

Satisfied, the stallion lowered his head. She felt warmth as wisps of breath floated between them.

He lipped her palm, tickling her fingers with a muzzle that was both whiskery and velvet. Sam let her breath out slowly, as he nudged her hand.

"Zanzibar, what do you want, boy?"

A faint brightness washed toward them. Without turning, Sam knew that either Dad or Gram had turned on the kitchen light. Probably checking on her at the worst possible moment.

The stallion shifted his weight between his two front hooves, aware of the change. The new light let her see the expression in his brown eyes. He was telling her something she was too dense to comprehend.

Sam's mind spun with choices. Was he investigating her as he would any unfamiliar object, or could he be asking her to pet him?

When his muzzle knocked against her wrist, Sam opened her fingers.

Mistake. The stallion acted as if she'd grown the claws of a cougar or bear. He was the Phantom once more. A savage light blazed in his eyes. He made a reckless swoop right, leading with a swing of his head. Heavy bone under smooth hide struck Sam's cheekbone. The impact knocked her off balance. Sam stumbled and drenched herself to the waist.

Headed for the safety of the range, the stallion swept past so near he might have trampled her, but he didn't. Sam wasn't grazed by even the edge of one hoof.

Rubbing her cheekbone, Sam watched him go. In his first instinctive burst of panic, the stallion had left the river, but once his hooves touched the riverbank, he moved more slowly. He loped a few rocking steps, then settled into a jog, mane and tail drifting as he left her.

Once he was out of sight, Sam felt cold. Her sweatpants sagged in a sodden effort to drag right off her hips and her toes felt so frozen, they might shatter as she dashed toward the house. At least they were numb, so she didn't feel the gravel's sting. Halfway to the house, she stopped, turned around and ran back to get her sleeping bag. Boy, it was a pain acting like a responsible kid.

Dad, wearing boots, jeans, and a half-buttoned flannel shirt, had the door open when Sam's feet hit the porch.

Dancing with cold, she slipped past him to land in a kitchen chair.

"Freezing, freezing, freezing," she said, then pulled

both feet up into her lap and rubbed them with her hands.

As she tried to knead warmth into her toes, Sam's mind was flooded with the wondrous thing that had happened. She looked up at Dad.

"I saw." Dad's hands rose and just hung in the air. Even though Dad was a man of few words, he used them well. Now, he seemed at a loss.

Sam swallowed hard, caught between crying and laughing. "Pretty amazing, huh?"

Dad nodded. "Was it the light that scared him off?"

So he'd seen her collision with the stallion. Sam had hoped he hadn't. She interlaced her fingers to keep from touching her face. Now that she was warming up, it hurt.

"No, it was my fault. I moved my hands in a weird way."

"And he knocked you down." The awe in Dad's face changed to concern.

"No, I get the blame for this," she said. As she stood, her wet pants made a puddle on the kitchen floor. "I tripped."

She faced her stubborn father. Were they about to clash, again?

"Mmm-hmm," Dad said. He slid the pad of his thumb along her cheekbone. "This is starting to swell. I think it's gonna bruise some."

"It doesn't hurt," Sam said. She made a point of

raising her chin. "And I wasn't a bit scared."

"He grew up real nice," Dad said, then let out a sigh and hung his thumbs in his jeans pockets. "You want something to eat?"

"No, I'm . . . " Sam stifled a yawn. The skin pulled tight where the stallion's head had struck her. "Just tired."

"Your head feels okay, except for that bump? I know Gram would keep you up a couple hours to watch for a concussion, but I'm inclined to let you get a good night's sleep."

"I'm fine, Dad. I took a lot harder hits when I got knocked on my booty playing basketball."

He smiled and Sam pressed her advantage.

"Can I—? Don't you think I should call Miss Olson in the morning and talk to her about Blackie?"

Dad frowned for a second before he shook his head.

"Time to discuss that tomorrow, Samantha. Now, get to bed."

Sam overslept.

Sunshine had painted her white walls yellow by the time she opened her eyes. She might not have awakened then if Gram hadn't brought a glass of orange juice to her bedside.

This time, when Sam yawned, it hurt.

"Oh dear, Wyatt was right." Gram clucked her tongue, eyes examining Sam's cheek.

"Don't touch it, please."

"Wouldn't think of it, dear, but you might want to borrow a little makeup," Gram sounded dubious, as if she wasn't convinced makeup was the solution.

Sam blinked. She hadn't worn makeup since she'd left San Francisco. Even then, she'd only worn a little mascara and lip gloss.

"Why?" Sam asked. "Does it look terrible?" She crawled out of bed to consult the mirror.

"You might be able to even out the color a little bit," Gram said. "Try it before you go outside."

Dad's truck idled in the yard and bolts rattled, but Sam didn't pay much attention. She stood in front of the mirror, wondering how a bump on the cheekbone had turned into this.

While Gram went to get the makeup, Sam studied the lumpy purplish distortion taking over the right side of her face. What fool had ever named this thing a simple "black eye"?

Gram returned and extended the bottle. "Do your best, honey, because if Jake sees that shiner, he's likely to have kittens."

A mask might have helped, but the makeup didn't. In fact, Sam thought the flesh-toned foundation made her look even more ready for Halloween.

So what if Jake was back? After twenty minutes of fussing with various combinations, she gave up, washed her face, put on a bright red tank top and white shorts and strode out into the ranch yard.

Jake had just loaded Pocahontas into a horse trailer. He turned, smiling, but just for a minute.

"You should see the other guy," Sam said, nearly shouting the phrase she'd rehearsed.

Jake didn't utter a sound. He fixed the metal doors tight behind the paint mare, then slid the bolts into place.

"Isn't that what men say, when they've got black eyes?" Sam kept a boasting tone in her voice.

Jake still faced the tailgate. "In case you hadn't noticed," he said, "you're not a man."

"Let it be, Jake." Dad moved to touch Jake's shoulder, then pulled his Stetson down a notch, instead. "She's fine."

Jake whirled around. His voice was low and hard to hear. "I leave for a couple days, and you get into trouble."

"I said, that's enough," Dad's voice grew stern. "I was watching her all along. If you'd been standing where she was, you'd be the one with the black eye."

"He may get one, yet," Sam taunted.

"That goes for you, too. Just hush," Dad snapped.

Sam crossed her arms. Jake shrugged. Both times he'd come close to defying Dad had been over her safety. And Dad let him get away with it, as if he and Jake were on the same team, or something. She wanted them both to knock it off.

"Gram and I are delivering this filly for Dawn

Archer's birthday," Dad said. "You kids take the day off. And sort this out however you want. Short of homicide."

Gram came hustling from the house and deposited a set of car keys dangling from a fluffy neon-green ball into Jake's hand.

"Jake, if there's an emergency or something, you can use the Buick, but be careful."

"Yes, ma'am," Jake said, but he gave Gram's boatlike yellow car the kind of sidelong glance horses gave rattlers.

As the truck and trailer pulled away from the ranch, Dad's arm waved through the driver's window. In a minute, it was across the River Bend bridge and gone, with only a line of dust to show it had passed.

"Well?" Jake said.

Now his arms were crossed and Sam's hands were on her hips, but she wasn't about to waste time fighting.

"Well, I'm going into the house and make a phone call my dad didn't tell me I *couldn't* make," Sam said. "And you, Jake Ely, can just suit yourself."

Chapter Fifteen ❧

Sᴀᴍ ꜱᴛᴏᴏᴅ ʙᴇꜱɪᴅᴇ the telephone, twirling the cord around her finger, tighter and tighter.

She'd already blurted out the details of her encounter with the Phantom to Jake, but telling a virtual stranger and expecting her to believe was going to be trickier.

Brynna Olson recognized Sam's voice at once, and she was being quite friendly, but Sam hadn't figured out how to tell the BLM employee that the Phantom was her horse. Jake, seated at the kitchen table with his chin propped on one hand, wasn't trying to make it easier.

"You've probably heard about the Phantom," Sam began. "He's sort of a local legend."

Jake made a face at that, so Sam turned toward the wall.

"Of course," Brynna's tone encouraged Sam. "The wild white stallion."

"Actually, the horse they're calling the Phantom now is a light gray with dapples. And—" Sam took a breath so deep, it might have fueled a dive into a bottomless sea. "He's my horse. Two years ago, my colt escaped and this is him."

Sam closed her eyes, wincing, ready for Miss Olson's laughter. Instead, she said the same thing Dad had. "You're sure?"

Sam opened her eyes, turned to Jake and gave him a victorious thumbs-up.

"I am sure, but there's no way to prove it. No papers, no recent photographs, no brand, tattoo, nothing." Sam waited.

And waited.

"Do you want to claim him?" Miss Olson asked.

"No. Well, sort of, but I just want him running free."

"If you *could* claim him, and keep him on your ranch lands, that'd be the best solution," Brynna spoke slowly, as if she were devising a plan. "Do you have his sire or dam, or any other domestic horses related to him?"

"Just a second, I'll check." Sam covered the phone's mouthpiece and repeated Brynna's question to Jake.

"I don't think so. Smoke's dead. Blackie was his last foal and your dad didn't breed him often."

"What about Kitty?" Sam asked, remembering

the flighty chestnut mare, Blackie's mother.

Jake made a dismissing motion. "Gone," he said, frowning.

"No luck," Sam said, but curiosity spurred her to see what Miss Olson had been considering. "What did you have in mind?"

"DNA testing," Brynna said. "Sounds pretty high tech for the Wild West, huh? But if the Phantom shared bloodlines with your domestic stock, that might be good enough. Still, those tests are a little pricey."

Sam thought of Aunt Sue's birthday money. "How pricey?"

"The lowest possible would be . . . oh shoot, about two thousand dollars."

Sam wondered if Jake saw her eyes bulge. Even if she could track down another of Smoke's foals, even if Dad developed a demented desire to adopt a wild stallion, they could not afford the tests.

"Samantha?" Brynna sounded as if she thought Sam might have fainted from shock. "It's unlikely we'll even bring him in. Why don't you relax?"

Sam had already disclosed everything except the location of the Phantom's valley, so she confessed her fear, too. "Because I think someone else will try to adopt him."

Papers rustled before Brynna asked, "Would that someone be Lincoln Slocum?"

"Yes." Sam slumped.

"Lincoln Slocum was in the parking lot this morning when I arrived at seven-thirty. He filled out adoption papers, saying he wanted to set things in motion, in case a horse came in that he liked." Brynna had resumed a cool, bureaucratic tone. "He expressed a particular interest in grays."

Sam held her free hand over her eyes. She longed to hand the telephone receiver to Jake and see if he could make this problem go away. But she knew he couldn't.

"That's really not good," Sam said.

"Don't give up. Just let me look at this application a minute . . ." Brynna's voice faded.

As Miss Olson looked over Slocum's application, Sam hoped the woman would find something that showed Slocum shouldn't be allowed to adopt a wild horse.

"Never mind," Brynna said. "To discuss this in any more detail would be unprofessional. I've only shared this much because the man annoyed me. He asked if he could finance a roundup targeting grays."

Sam thought a second. A helicopter, pilot, wranglers, trailers, and portable corrals were, as Brynna said, pretty pricey. "He wanted to pay for it all? Himself?"

Sam heard the sound of an open hand slamming a desktop.

"Can you believe it?" Brynna's voice soared with

outrage. "Of course, I told him the federal government doesn't work that way, and then—" Brynna turned businesslike again. "Samantha, please give me your number, so I can phone if there are any developments which might interest you."

Sam had barely finished reciting the numbers, when the woman said, "You have a nice day."

"Wait, wait! Brynna?"

"Yes, Samantha," Brynna's patience sounded strained.

"I think one of Linc Slocum's cowboys is working for you."

In the moment of silence, Sam couldn't tell if Brynna was perturbed with her or if she resented the possibility that she'd been used.

"We always have new hires in the summer—" Brynna began.

"His name's Flick."

"—but thank goodness, no one by that name."

And then Brynna Olson hung up.

"I guess I am glad you're back," Sam admitted, after she'd shared the bad news with Jake. "Where were you, anyway?"

"My mom had to drive into Reno for a teachers' conference. It's to help rural teachers keep up with the rest of the state."

Gram had mentioned Jake's mother taught at Darton High School. Sam was eager to see her again and glad she'd know a teacher at her new school, even if her only memory of Maxine Ely was a small blond woman as vivacious as her Shosone husband was quiet.

"It's about a four-hour trip, and Mom thought I could use the driving practice. In fact, I tested for my license while I was there. And passed." Jake looked smug.

"Now, if you only had a car," she teased.

"You sure know how to make a guy feel important, Sam. Someday you'll ask me to take you someplace and I'll remind you of that crack.

"Anyway, since Mom had a hotel room to herself and Dad won't leave the ranch unless it's for a wedding or funeral, I went and hung around."

"Doing what?" Sam asked.

"The hotel had a gym and swimming pool, and a video arcade. Mainly, I watched a lot of TV."

Sam didn't feel a single twinge of jealousy, but she did feel relieved and her sigh escaped in a gust.

"Your eye hurt?" Jake guessed.

"No," Sam said, though it was sore and she didn't like being reminded of how it must look. "I thought Dad had fired you."

"Fired me?" Jake laughed. "I guess he could, but that's not really how we work. It's more like, we both make a small profit and a big reputation for turning out good, gentle working horses.

"We go to auctions, buy raw horses, then school them."

"Like Pocahontas," Sam said. "Weren't you sorry to see her go?"

"A little, but Dawn Archer's a good rider, and her dad's had his eye on that filly from the first. He'll pay Wyatt top dollar, now that she's gentled. And that's how it works. When we sell, your dad deducts the horse's price, the cost of feed, shots and shoes, and then we split the profit—sixty percent for him and forty percent for me."

"It won't be enough to buy a car, will it?" Sam asked.

"It all adds up," Jake said, rubbing his hands together like a miser. "And it beats working at McDonald's or Phil's Fill-Up."

The ringing phone startled them. It was too soon for Dad and Gram to be calling to check on them, and ranchers didn't hang around the house talking on the phone in the middle of the morning.

"Hello?"

"Samantha, this is Brynna Olson. We have that stallion."

"Now? But I thought you said—"

"Two of our new hires just brought him in crosstied and blindfolded. They said they got a complaint from a nearby rancher," Brynna sounded doubtful. "What matters is this: the horse seemed pretty calm until they removed this black sweater they'd used to blindfold him. Once he saw where he was, that stallion started screaming. He went insane."

"Oh, no."

"Samantha, this is serious. He's rammed a wooden fence. He's bleeding and we can't get close to him. He's reared and gone over backward. Other horses are panicking. A foal may have broken her leg trying to escape. This is serious," she repeated.

Sam didn't allow her heart to break. The Phantom had been tricked and betrayed. She was his only hope.

"I'll be there as soon as I can," she promised.

"I hope it's soon enough." Brynna's no-nonsense voice was colder than ever. "Because if I can't get him sedated, I'll have to put him down."

Jake grabbed Gram's fluffy key chain before Sam could explain. He went out to start the Buick while Sam scrawled a note to Dad and Gram, grabbed her purple pages, then ran after him. She had to jump back on the porch, though, when the car careened too close.

"Can you drive this thing? Or—"

"Or what?" Jake demanded.

"Or—" Sam climbed in and buckled her seat belt, then wrapped her arms around her ribs as they bumped toward the bridge. The big car didn't look like it would fit. "Or should I see if I can get Dallas to drive me up there? I mean, you barely have your license."

"No kidding?" Jake accelerated once they crossed

the bridge. "And after you found Dallas, do you really think he'd figure this was enough of an emergency to quit working on the pump after he told Wyatt he'd handle it?" Jake filled the silence. "I don't think so."

Jake was right. He was also risking a lot by driving Gram's car with a brand-new license. Sam wondered why he hadn't hesitated to take her to the aid of a horse he feared would hurt her. He must be doing this for her.

"Thanks, Jake."

He grunted and kept driving.

They drove ten minutes without passing another car and Sam stayed quiet so Jake could concentrate. They slipped through Alkali without slowing down.

Sam wondered if Slocum was in front of them or behind them. Only when they made the hard right turn off the asphalt and onto the dirt road that would take them uphill to Thread the Needle and the Willow Springs corral did she find out.

Jake sucked in a breath that made Sam worry.

She bit her lip as rocks crunched under the Buick's tires. The big car wallowed a minute before holding upright on the dirt road.

"We doing okay?" she asked.

"Fine, but you'd better keep watch out the back window. I just caught a glimpse of Slocum's car."

The tan Cadillac was about a mile behind them.

"He's an adult," Sam blurted.

"So?"

"Neither of us can sign for the adoption."

"Sam, we're not going to adopt the Phantom. We're driving up there to, uh, to try to—just why *are* we going?"

"To keep him from getting hurt."

"Don't tell me you think you can get close to him like you did last night." He glanced away from the road and gave her a grim glare. "Do not tell me that."

Sam stared out the windshield. That's exactly what she planned to do. But Jake had said not to tell him, so she wouldn't.

"Sam? Better answer me, or I'm pulling over right now and waving Slocum good luck as he goes past."

"I'm just going because Brynna said I should," Sam said and it was only a white lie. Brynna must have wanted her to come, or she wouldn't have called.

Jake swerved around a refrigerator-sized rock. "She has to hold horses 'til they've been freeze-branded and vaccinated, anyway."

Jake was trying to comfort her, but as Sam shrank back against the seat, she imagined the Phantom's terror. And though the branding and vaccinating would hurt the stallion, it wouldn't hurt as much as the betrayal. For the first time since she'd hung up the phone, Sam thought about the blindfold Brynna had described.

"You know that they used my sweater to blindfold him?"

"Yeah?" Jake sawed at the steering wheel as they began a series of switchbacks. "That was a dirty trick."

"They used *my* scent to keep him calm. That flash I saw on the ridge last night was probably Slocum, smoking cigarettes and throwing matches like he always does." Sam shivered. Like a stalker, Slocum had been watching her.

"It means Slocum started planning this a long time ago, during the cattle drive. That's when my sweater disappeared. He's a weird guy, Jake."

"He's also a fast guy," Jake said, eyes on the rearview mirror.

Sam twisted to look over the seat back. Slocum was gaining on them. "Can Gram's car go any faster?"

"Not much, but I have an idea."

Jake punched the accelerator and the car wobbled too near the edge of the road, but they drew away, steadily. They'd almost reached Thread the Needle and the Cadillac was just slogging through the switchbacks.

As Gram's car entered the single-lane road, Jake slammed on the brakes.

"What are you doing?" Sam shouted. Since last time, she'd had a creepy feeling about Thread the Needle. "You said there's no way another car can pass here. You can't stop."

But Jake did stop. He switched off the ignition

and left the car aslant the road. He climbed out, fiddled with the hood, and opened it.

Sam climbed out, too. The desert heat hit her as if she'd opened the world's biggest oven door. For an instant she was glad to be dressed in shorts and tennis shoes instead of boots and jeans.

Then she watched Jake's head disappear under the car hood.

"Jake?"

"Quit shrieking and start running, Brat." His voice was muffled. "I'm pulling out the"—he stretched further into the engine compartment and tugged— "coil to the distributor. My buddy Darrell . . ." he began, then changed what he'd been about to say, "is someone you don't need to meet, but he always has a trick up his sleeve and this is one he taught me."

With a satisfied sound, Jake reappeared. He shoved a wire, curled like a spring, at her.

"Stick that in your pocket," Jake ordered. "Gram's Buick isn't going anywhere until we put it back."

The Cadillac roared closer. Sam hated to leave Jake to deal with an angry and frustrated Slocum.

"Run, Sam!" Jake gave Sam a shove between the shoulder blades, and she took off. "And don't do anything stupid!"

Chapter Sixteen ஒ

SAM'S HEARTBEAT pounded in her throat, in her arms, and in her face. It wasn't the blistering heat that made her run a choppy pace. Sam was afraid.

She slipped on a patch of gravel. Her feet shot out from under her body and only her hands kept her face from slamming into the dirt.

Sam stood, wiped the dirt and blood from her palms on her shorts, and glanced down the hillside to her left.

Hypnotized by the steep drop-off, Sam couldn't help but look. Far away, River Bend was arranged like a toy ranch and the river glinted silver-blue.

If only the Phantom were down there, playing in the river, safe and sound. But he wasn't, so Sam kept running.

If Slocum got her horse, there were ways to get him back. If Zanzibar died . . .

She quit thinking of the powerful stallion, slamming

the door on those nightmare images. Instead, she thought of Jake. Slocum had probably reached him by now. Slocum would be furious. But Jake was younger, stronger, and faster. And hard in a way Slocum could never achieve, even if he spent hours in a gym. Jake worked. Slocum only pretended. Slocum had to buy the trappings of a cowboy. Jake was the real thing.

The rhythm of Sam's steps turned regular. She caught her breath, kept her head level, and aimed her eyes straight ahead.

She heard the Phantom's neigh, before she saw him. Raspy, as if he'd screamed his throat raw, his cry and galloping hooves lured Sam to his corral.

People. Sam caught a glimpse of Miss Olson in her khaki-colored uniform. She saw Flick and the men she'd identified as Bale Thrower and Clipboard when she'd visited the corrals before. She refused to let them see her. Or stop her.

Sam ducked and sneaked along the fence, keeping her head low. She couldn't risk walking to the gate and opening it. If Phantom galloped through, he'd be lost in the maze of corrals and easily recaptured. She looked for another way in.

Down a few yards, a bottom rail was missing from the fence. She crept along, determined to reach that gap. Once there, she'd slip under and into the corral before she was spotted.

"The vet's on her way."

Sam recognized Miss Olson's voice. Her tone was so unemotional, Sam couldn't tell if the vet was coming to sedate the stallion or destroy him.

As if he understood, the stallion trumpeted a challenging neigh. Sam had to look. She crouched and peered through the fence rails.

The Phantom was transformed by fury. Dirt dulled his silver coat. His drifting mane lay clumped and matted with mud from dust mixed with his sweat, but he fought captivity with every weapon a wild horse possessed.

He tried speed, galloping around the corral. Stumbling and exhausted, he still tried to outrun the walls surrounding him.

He tried slashing hooves, battering the fence until he dropped back, all four legs spread wide to keep from falling.

He tried screaming with defiance. He was a king of stallions determined to scare his captor.

And then, once more, he ran.

"I want to see you two, now," Miss Olson's voice snapped with authority. She stood with one foot on the porch. From where Sam hid, it looked like there was a pile of rope on the porch. Sam hoped Miss Olson was calling in the two men who'd trapped the Phantom.

"Yeah?" The lazy voice was Flick's. "Ed's gone, but what do you want with me?"

He didn't sound worried. Miss Olson's voice was

stern, but Sam didn't have time to listen.

Time was running out. Sam edged closer to the gap beneath the fence.

The faltering stutter of the Phantom's hooves made Sam wonder if the stallion scented her. His dread increased. He ran faster, streaking along the fence line and slamming into a corner. Only then did he turn, run, and ram into the next corner.

Blood ran between his churning forelegs. Twists of forelock hid his eyes, but that wasn't why he kept running and slamming into each corner. The royal stallion ran blind with rage.

"He's doing it again," Miss Olson sounded close. "I'm afraid he'll run himself to death."

There were mumbles from Bale Thrower and Clipboard, but Sam heard Flick clearly.

"Hasn't got a brain left in that puny mustang head," Flick said.

"You've got your paycheck," Miss Olson said. "I asked you to leave. Do it."

"Oh yes, ma'am." Flick laughed. "I guess I got what I came for."

Sam knew he didn't mean the money.

Face lowered to within a quarter inch of the dirt, Sam slid under the fence rails. The stallion's hooves came to a halt.

Sam stood. If anyone saw her now, it would be too late. She walked slowly to the middle of the corral. The stallion watched, vibrating with an emotion Sam couldn't read.

This wasn't the river. None of the stallion's movements would be slowed by water. Sam's cheek still ached from last night's accidental blow.

If this horse wanted to hurt her, she couldn't stop him.

If he hurt her, Miss Olson would surely put him down.

With everything at stake, Sam stretched out her hand in a gesture the horse understood.

The stallion froze. His nostrils flared wide from exertion. Sam imagined the feel of velvet muzzle and prickly whiskers, but the stallion didn't lower his head as he had last night.

He straightened to a commanding height, tossed his forelock back, and stared. He blinked once, as if he couldn't believe she'd dare this.

He took two steps forward and as he did, Sam heard Miss Olson gasp. She said something, too, but Sam quit listening as the Phantom pinned back his ears and charged.

Sam didn't move, couldn't move, and the stallion passed by. Dust choked her, but she refused to cough. His hooves stamped behind her, and she turned to face him.

Sam reached into her memory, trying to recall the signs of horse language Jake had taught her.

The stallion reared, showing a vast underbelly spattered with mud and blood. He lowered to all four legs, gathered himself into a churning coil of muscle, and charged past again, head snaking out as if he'd bite; but he didn't.

The stallion told her he was confused and angry. He said he wasn't going to kill her, even if she deserved it.

He moved around the pen at a trot and as he turned gracefully at each corner, Sam sighed. The Phantom was acting like a normal, nervous horse.

Voices attracted her eyes.

Jake was there. "She knows what she's doing. At least *he* thinks she does."

The stallion curved away from the fence and walked toward her. He stopped and stared toward the mountains, with one ear turned her way.

Sam talked to him.

"Hey boy, I'm sorry. I'm so sorry they hurt you."

The horse shuddered, but his ear stayed turned to catch each word. She knew the sound he was waiting for and she uttered it so quietly, no one else could hear.

"Zanzibar," Sam breathed the word, hoping it reached his ears.

Her scent had betrayed the stallion. The word was all she had left to offer him. The word held all her love. No one else must hear it. Ever.

The stallion's head swung to face her. He took two steps, then pawed the dirt. His respiration was labored, raising his wide chest. Blood misted from his nostrils.

"Zanzibar," she whispered. "It's okay. I'll get you out of here, I will."

When his lips fluttered, Sam felt his breath. His neck stretched past her hand, lifting. If he bolted now, she'd go down under his hooves to be trampled.

"Zanzibar, I love you, big horse."

The stallion lowered his mighty head to Sam's shoulder. His sigh rocked them both. She saw his muscles loosen, felt his head grow heavy as he calmed.

Neither horse nor girl moved, for a very long time.

Slocum's high-heeled boots and broad belly kept him from reaching Willow Springs until after Sam left the Phantom resting in his corral.

As Sam came through the gate, Jake called her nine kinds of fool and ten kinds of idiot, then gave her a hug that nearly broke her ribs.

Miss Olson ordered Sam to sit down on the office stairs, until she decided whether to arrest her or award her a medal. Sam gave Miss Olson the purple pages, just in case they could sway things in her favor. The woman skimmed them, folded them into her pocket, but didn't comment on Sam's hours of work.

When Slocum finally staggered up to the porch

outside the office, he was puffing from exertion, but doing his best to seem polite.

"Miss Olson," Slocum took her hand in a meaty grip. "I hardly expected to see you again so soon. But it's a pleasure, of course." Slocum paused to breathe. "Excuse me," he said, patting his chest. "I walked all the way up here. Some old clunker of a car broke down on the road and its driver neglected to pull over to the side."

Slocum glared at Jake, then continued, "I hear you were able to recapture my horse."

"*Your* horse?" Sam shot up from her seat on the porch. "What in the world are you talking about?"

"Oh now, sugar," Slocum said, hefting his belt so the trophy buckle dented his overhanging belly. "You're not hoping that's your little black colt all grown up and changed color, are you?" Slocum gave Miss Olson a just-us-adults smile, then studied Sam more closely. "What happened to your eye, Samantha? Didn't sass Wyatt, did you?"

The insinuation that her father would hit her was like pouring gasoline on Sam's already flaming anger.

"Unlike some people, my father never hurts anyone or anything," Sam shouted. "And he"—she pointed toward the corral— "is not your horse."

Miss Olson made a smoothing motion with her hands.

Jake tugged at her elbow.

"Fire coming out of your nostrils there, Brat,"

Jake said quietly. "Take it easy. I think the law's on your side."

He probably meant Miss Olson, but she wasn't "the law," just a government representative. Still, the redhead's icy expression said she was in control. Sam sat down.

"Miss Olson and I have already talked about the matter of the gray's scar," Slocum said.

Sam met Jake's eyes. If Miss Olson had read Sam's notes, she'd know how folks said Phantom had gotten that scar.

"And I told Mr. Slocum I couldn't accept it as proof of ownership. If I could accept circumstantial evidence, I'd be inclined to award him to Samantha. She has an amazing link with that stallion."

Sam tried to catch Miss Olson's eye, to thank her for the compliment, but the woman didn't seem interested.

"I suppose she demonstrated some of Jake Ely's Indian mumbo jumbo," Slocum scoffed.

Miss Olson left enough silence that even Slocum looked embarrassed. Then she went on.

"As a horsewoman, I was convinced by what I saw. It was better than a bill of sale. As a representative of the federal government, however, it's not good enough."

The redhead leaned against the porch railing with her arms crossed. Even then, her crisp uniform didn't wrinkle. As always, Miss Olson looked detached, but something told Sam the woman was waiting for Slocum to stumble into a trap.

Sam decided to give him a push.

"Mr. Slocum, did you make the complaint about the Phantom?" Sam asked.

"A complaint? Must be some misunderstanding. I did call." Slocum rocked back on his bootheels. "The horse was on my property, and I could've just put my rope on him—"

"Like you did before," Sam nudged him to admit it.

"—but I wanted everything to be official, this time."

This time. Bingo. Slocum had just admitted he'd caught the stallion before. Wasn't that illegal?

Sam kept herself from looking at Miss Olson.

Slocum could go to jail for that. Sam was sure of it. She pressed her lips together. It wouldn't do to crow with delight.

But Slocum wasn't stupid. He turned shame-faced toward Miss Olson. "I used to have a cowboy who fancied himself a buckaroo. He caught the stallion, once." Slocum looked down at his eel-skin boots and shook his head. "Tempted as I was, I wouldn't keep him. After all, it's against the law."

Jake had heard enough. "Then how come you offered me two hundred bucks to track him down for you?"

"What *are* you talking about, Jake?" He winked at Miss Olson. "These kids."

"They can really get some crazy ideas," she said. "Still, I can't help wondering why you didn't report the harassment of a wild horse. That's a prohibited act under the Wild Free-Roaming Horse and Burro Act of 1971."

Yes, Sam thought.

Slocum only slowed down a minute, then answered, "I wanted to give the young man a chance."

"Even though you knew the horse was bleeding." Miss Olson pretended to wince. "That would count as negligence, another prohibited act."

"Miss Olson, it's not something I like to talk about, but you and I both know horses can bleed all day long and—"

"And you'd noticed the animal's injuries were severe enough to scar."

"If I'd thought he was suffering, dang it, I would have put him out of his misery," Slocum snapped.

"Without permission of an authorized officer?" Miss Olson shook her head. "Another prohibited act."

Snorting like a bull, Slocum dropped all pretense of cooperation. "Lady, you can take your prohibited acts and—"

"Go to court with them, Mr. Slocum?" Miss Olson smiled.

"In that adoption application, you can read that the commission of prohibited acts are punishable by a two-thousand-dollar fine or a year in prison. That's for each offense." Miss Olson pretended to calculate. "And how many are we up to now?"

"Three!" Sam said, counting the charges on her fingers. "Harassment, negligence, and destruction, right, Jake?"

"I'm no expert," Jake said. He nodded toward Miss Olson.

"Mr. Slocum, until I have time to do a background check, I'm deferring your application to adopt a wild horse."

Slocum sputtered. "You can't—I'm gonna— When I—" He started three sentences and they all fizzled out. Finally, he shouted, "I have connections in Washington!"

"Do you?" Miss Olson looked bored. "The fact remains, you need to leave the premises, until you're more relaxed."

"I'm not leaving." Slocum paced up and down. He glanced at Bale Thrower with a little concern, then got his courage up. "You're not a cop, Olson, and you can't make me."

Bale Thrower and Clipboard walked a step closer. Jake crossed his arms, looking ready for a fight.

"I could make a citizen's arrest." Sam heard the words tumble from her lips and wondered where they'd come from.

When Slocum sneered, Miss Olson said, "I don't think that will be necessary, Samantha. Hugh, perhaps you'd give Mr. Slocum a ride back to his car."

So, the big man Sam had been thinking of as "Bale Thrower" was really named Hugh. He stepped forward with a grin. He'd obviously enjoyed this showdown with Slocum.

Frustrated, Slocum swept off his cowboy hat and hit it against his leg, as he'd seen real cowboys do. Then he pointed at Sam.

"This isn't over, Samantha Forster." He pulled his hat back on. "It is *not* over."

Chapter Seventeen ⌒

$\mathscr{I}$F SHE DIDN'T COUNT the time her first grade teacher had told her to stop reading storybooks during arithmetic *or else*, Sam had never been threatened by an adult.

Slocum's threat had scared her. She was safe now, with Jake and Miss Olson standing by, but what about later?

Sam's hands still shook after Miss Olson disappeared into her office with a promise of lunch.

"Citizen's arrest, huh?"

"Shut up, Jake. It worked, didn't it?" Sam gave him a shove.

Jake's broad shoulders barely moved.

"No kidding, Brat. *I* was terrified."

Sam giggled. The laughter felt good, but it only lasted until Miss Olson came back. She balanced a cell phone between her cheek and shoulder and placed sodas and a box of crackers on the porch between Jake and Sam.

Miss Olson broke off her conversation for a moment. "Is your dad home?" she asked.

"No," Sam said.

Shaking her head, Miss Olson turned away, still talking.

Sam didn't mean to eavesdrop, but she heard words like "stallion," "local girl," and "restraining order."

Sam ate one saltine, then another. When she'd eaten half a dozen and sipped down half of her sugary soda, she felt better.

With a beep, Miss Olson folded her cell phone, strolled back to the porch, and sat near Sam and Jake.

"You outsmarted him, Samantha," Miss Olson sounded pleased, but a cautious tone lingered in her voice.

"Please call me Sam," she said. "When you say Samantha, it sounds like I'm in trouble."

"You may be, but not from me." Miss Olson extended her arm for a handshake. "I'll call you Sam if you agree to call me Brynna."

They shook. Brynna looked up at Jake's grunt of discomfort.

"Something wrong, Mr. Ely?"

"Naw," Jake said. "I just want to hear what kind of trouble Sam's in."

Brynna sighed. "Linc Slocum didn't like Sam

outsmarting him. He knows no one around here would take his part against her."

"Unless he paid them," Jake said. "Like he paid Flick."

"Right," Brynna said. "Wherever he came from, Slocum could buy what he wanted. In that way, he's different from folks around here. They work for what they want."

"Besides that, he's sneaky," Sam said.

"Right," Brynna agreed. "Even though most Nevada ranchers can't stand the BLM"—Brynna held her hand palm out to Sam and Jake as they shifted—"and we won't discuss why—the fact remains they're straightforward about their complaints. Slocum lied about the horse. When that didn't work, he gave intimidation a try. And that failed, too.

"I don't think he'll hurt you, Sam, but I think it would be wise to make provisions for the stallion. Right away."

Sam's mind spun. What would be best for the Phantom?

"I bet Wyatt would let you adopt him, if we told him what happened," Jake said.

"It's a good thing he wasn't here," Sam said. She'd never seen Dad hurt anyone, but Sam could imagine him slugging Slocum for threatening her.

"Slocum's approach would have been entirely different if Mr. Forster were here," Brynna said, but she refused to be led off the topic. "The afternoon's creeping away from us. We need to help that horse."

Both Jake and Brynna stared at Sam, waiting. And that wasn't the worst of it. The Phantom yearned for the open range and his herd. By placing his head upon her shoulder, he'd said he trusted her to help. If only she knew how.

Jake rubbed the back of his neck, frowning, but Brynna looked eager.

"Any suggestions?" Sam encouraged her.

"Just one, but I think it's a winner." Brynna drew a deep breath. "BLM doesn't put all captured horses up for adoption. We release some because we think there's little chance they'd find a home. Others"— Brynna paused—"we release to enrich existing herds."

Jake must be following Brynna's suggestion faster than she was, because Sam didn't understand why Jake began reciting Blackie's pedigree.

"His sire was pure mustang, but his dam is Princess Kitty, a running Quarter horse with Three Bars breeding on one side and King Leo on the other."

Brynna and Jake stared at each other as if they were designing a conspiracy.

Slowly, Sam puzzled out Brynna's idea, aloud. "So, you're saying you—"

"The BLM," Brynna corrected.

"Okay, the BLM could turn the Phantom loose?

Because his colts and fillies would improve the wild herds, they'd set him free? Just like that?"

"Just like that," Brynna said. "I've already checked with one of our wild horse specialists, and verified the gray's herd is the only viable band in the Calico Mountains district. There are a few bachelor bands—young stallions who roam together without mares—but those stallions are small and scrubby. If they took over the gray's herd, we'd end up with fewer adoptable horses."

"Let's do it," Sam said. "Slocum won't have a chance to cause any more trouble."

Brynna didn't look so sure, but she made a promise. "As long as I'm manager here, Slocum won't get a single wild horse."

"I hate to rain on your parade," Jake said. "But we can't just set him loose. Think of the fences between here and the mountains and," he gestured, "the cars coming up that road."

"It's a long truck ride back to the Calicos, but we could trailer him there and release him," Brynna suggested.

Sam imagined the tight, moving world within a horse trailer. The Phantom had fought the corral as if locked in a death match. Would he survive hours in a trailer?

Jake must have thought the same thing.

"If you could get him as far as Thread the Needle," he suggested, "I bet he'd head downhill toward River Bend."

In minutes, Brynna and Jake spun out a plan while Sam listened.

The stallion had been halterbroken as a foal. And the stallion trusted Ace.

After seeing Sam with the Phantom, Jake believed she could ride Ace and lead the stallion to Thread the Needle.

"I'll go back for Ace," Jake said. "I need to move Gram's Buick, anyway."

As Sam worked the coiled car part out of her pocket and handed it to Jake, Brynna stared at it, confused.

"I don't want to know," Brynna said, when Sam started to explain.

"Wyatt's sure to be back with the trailer by the time I get there," Jake said. "Do we need anything besides Ace and a lead rope?"

"I've got plenty of rope," Brynna said. "It'd be best if Sam started working him with the halter, right now."

Things were moving too fast. Sam wasn't sure the stallion would recall his halter training. Even if he did, why should he obey?

Sam watched Jake leave. Then, gingerly, she touched her cheekbone. It hurt. And her brain felt like mush. She was probably just tired. Once she slipped back into the Phantom's pen, she'd probably remember how to think like a horse.

There was only one way to find out.

With a soft rope halter and lead, Sam walked to the Phantom's pen. The stallion stood opposite the gate, body hugging the fence. His ears flicked at the sound of the gate opening. Otherwise, he didn't move.

Sam entered the corral. He ignored her.

"Hey boy," she crooned, but for each step she took closer, the stallion moved a step away. He must have listened for each footfall, because he never looked at Sam.

Sam talked and talked. After a while, she spoke not to the stallion, but to Brynna.

"You're an expert. Tell me, why do people want wild horses?"

"Some want to help them, of course—"

"No, I mean, you've read all the old West stories," Sam said. "For hundreds of years, people have wanted wild horses."

"They look at a wild horse and see beauty, spirit—"

"And they can't wait to take it away," Sam interrupted.

She saw the new rope burns on the stallion's neck and realized he wouldn't willingly let her halter him. But what else could she do?

For two hours, Sam followed the stallion around the enclosure. He never broke into a run, never battered the rails as he had before, and never gave a sign that he heard her speak his secret name.

At last, Sam sat down with her back against the fence. The position was dangerous and she knew it. If the stallion decided to charge, she couldn't move fast enough to escape. But trust must run two ways. Maybe he'd come to her.

A shiver ran over the stallion's body. Keeping his head turned her way, he edged toward the water bucket, lowered his head and drank deeply. His eyes remained fixed on Sam and she realized they weren't brown and lively, now, but black and questioning.

The stallion hadn't given up hope. He was waiting for her to understand.

She watched every twitch of muscle, every movement of his lips, every shifting of his weight from leg to leg. Even when Dad and Jake arrived, she didn't stop.

"I do not believe what I'm seeing," Dad's voice was low and furious. "Tell me that is not my daughter in a pen—*sitting* in a pen with a wild stallion."

Brynna answered, but Sam blocked out their conversation. She kept watching the Phantom. It seemed the water had revitalized him.

"Okay," she said softly to the stallion. "Okay, I'm getting it."

And then he made sure she understood.

Tossing his mane and forelock in fanfare, the stallion lifted his muzzle and pranced toward the fence. He gazed toward the mountains and uttered a neigh of longing.

Hooves stamped in the confinement of the River Bend horse trailer and Ace answered with a short burst of whinnies.

In spite of the danger, in spite of what Dad and Jake and Brynna might say, Sam knew what she must do. She walked toward the gate.

"Our idea's not going to work," Sam said, closing the corral gate behind her.

"You are testing my patience, Sam," Dad said, but his arm draped over her like a bird's sheltering wing.

Sam hugged him back, but didn't let the warmth of Dad's welcome slow her down.

"When Flick and the other guy dragged the Phantom in here, cross-tied, they—I don't know, traumatized him, I think. He's not going to let me halter him or pony him with Ace. And he won't go into the trailer. But I know what *will* work."

"I'm listening," Jake said, but his thumbs were in his jeans pockets and he looked at the dirt, not her.

Sam's stomach dropped away, as if she were rising in a fast elevator, before she said, "We wait until dark."

"Oh, no," Dad crossed his arms.

"I don't know why, but he trusts me more in the dark," she said. "Then Ace and I run toward Thread the Needle, and start down the hillside toward River Bend. Just like we were going to, only—"

"Only you don't pony him, you use Ace like a

Judas horse." Brynna spoke with a kind of dread, but she understood.

"Yes."

Sam had read how the BLM trapped wild horses, using a keyhole-shaped corral. The mustangs came running, herded by a helicopter, and then, at the last minute, just as the horses might sense the opening to the trap, a domestic horse, who knew a bucket of grain awaited inside, was released. As he ran for his treat, the mustangs followed and the gate closed behind them.

"Only Ace isn't a Judas horse," Sam said. "He's the Phantom's guardian angel, because he's going to lead him out of here."

"And you'll be riding Ace," Jake said.

"Yeah," she admitted.

"That's all fine, but let's go back to the part where you gallop downhill in the dark and break your fool neck!" Jake kept his voice level, until he turned toward Dad. "Wyatt, are you going to let her do this?"

"Dad, I'll only run him there," Sam pointed at the straight road, smoothed by car traffic. "When we reach the hillside, I won't gallop. I'll leave the pace up to Ace.

"Remember what you taught me? He doesn't want to fall. He wants to keep his four legs underneath him. Isn't that what you've always said, Dad?"

Sam crossed her arms. Dad crossed his.

To Brynna, Dad must look more intimidating. With her hacked-off hair, black eye, sunburned arms, and legs dirty from sitting in a dusty horse corral, Sam knew she didn't look as determined as she felt.

But Jake knew her. He walked away, reached a hand into the horse trailer toward Ace, and left the standoff to the two Forsters.

In the deepening dusk, Sam saw Dad shake his head.

"You could get hurt again," he said.

Sam heard his fear. It made her feel selfish, but she had to do this for her horse.

"Dad, I don't want to get hurt. I don't want to go back to the hospital or to San Francisco. I want to stay here, with you and Gram." She looked toward the horse trailer. "And Jake. But I want to do what's right."

Dad glanced through the fence rails. The stallion looked weary and harmless in the gray failing light.

"I haven't told you this before, Sam, but when you're absolutely sure of something, you look a lot like your mom. She'd get convinced she knew what to do, and usually, she turned out convincing me, too. Like keeping the ranch," Dad said quietly. "Like having a child."

A sweet warmth enveloped Sam. The sun had vanished behind the mountains and the sky had turned dark blue.

"I say it's close enough to dark," Dad said. "Jake, bring Ace out."

On the high road overlooking Willow Springs, Sam crouched in the saddle while Ace danced beneath her.

Down below, metal slammed as Brynna opened a series of interconnecting gates, funneling the stallion toward the road. At first, the Phantom was slow and cautious.

Then he understood. His legs moved more quickly, picking up speed, trotting faster, until his hooves hammered like gunfire as he came closer and closer.

"Now!" Jake shouted.

Sam clapped her heels to Ace's sides. He leaped forward as the final gate clanged open.

"Go on, Blackie!" Dad yelled.

Behind her, the stallion's hooves stuttered, held and raced after them.

Sam's heart echoed the thunder of hoofbeats. Both horses breathed loud with excitement, and then the Phantom ran beside them, beautiful once more.

How far left to gallop along this road? Sam knew she had to judge. A half mile? A quarter?

The Phantom held his head high, all senses alert. Eyes wide, nostrils open, he tested the breeze for anything other than sagebrush and juniper. He could have passed them, any time, but he matched strides with Ace, loping with long-legged care, unsure of the earth beneath his hooves.

At Thread the Needle, they slowed.

"Take us home, Ace," Sam said.

She leaned back a little, balancing so Ace could pick his way down the hillside.

The Phantom's warm hide rubbed Sam's leg. Even though the men with ropes had fractured her friendship with the stallion, a link remained.

The stallion ran headlong into darkness with a girl and a small outcast mustang as his guides.

A warm updraft of wind brought the green scent of the river. The lights of River Bend ranch were no more than a mile away, when the stallion surged ahead.

He left her.

Silent, except for night wind rushing through his mane and tail, the stallion ran, stretching so his belly brushed the ground.

Carefully, Sam drew rein. Ace slowed. They couldn't catch the stallion. The little gelding didn't try. His home was a place among fences, with plenty of water, and a snug, straw-deep stall when the snows came.

The Phantom crashed into the river. Waves surged for the shore.

At the water's edge, she slid from Ace's back and left him ground-tied as she waded in up to her knees, watching the stallion go.

He gained the other shore and shook the water

from his coat. Moonlight turned the droplets into silver dust.

The Phantom whirled, sighting everything around him, assuring himself of safety. Then, he made a graceful leap toward the mountains and freedom.

With each of the stallion's steps Sam felt reality settle around her. Her horse was gone for good.

Summer's magic had ended with Jake's anger, Slocum's threats, and a wild stallion running. Between now and September, she had an unfamiliar school, with Slocum's snobbish children, left to dread.

And then Ace snorted and stared into a darkness with only a twinkling of starlight to show the stallion swinging a wide turn back.

Sam ran, splashing through the river shallows. The current held her back, warning her the water flow was too strong to test. She couldn't go to him, and the stallion had turned too wary to come to her.

He stopped, knee-deep in silver water. His reflection wavered on the rills and ripples. Since they were alone, Sam shouted.

"Zanzibar!"

The stallion rose into the air, rearing as if his forelegs reached for the moon. Sam understood his neigh as if he'd spoken. From the wild side of the river, the Phantom promised to return.

From

Phantom Stallion

∽❦ ❦∾

MUSTANG MOON

On the ridge above them stood Hammer and Sweetheart. Hammer sampled the wind, searching for the scent of a stallion that might interfere with his plan. His mane flapped as his head bobbed in satisfaction, and then he was running.

The stallion stampeded down the trail, nipping at Sweetheart's heels as she ran with him. By the time she saw what had frightened Strawberry, Sam was falling.

Sam had almost regained her seat when Strawberry slipped, clambered upright, then made for open ground. The mare's serpentine gallop kept Sam from settling into the saddle. She sagged to the right.

Suddenly, Strawberry gave a seesawing buck, then another.

Sam grabbed for the horn, but it wasn't enough. She wouldn't be able to ride this out, especially if Hammer moved in close. Sam refused to surrender Strawberry to Hammer. It was time to act, but she didn't know the right thing to do.

An experienced cowgirl would stay in the saddle,

but if Strawberry bolted again, Sam knew she'd fall. Instead, she slid down Strawberry's left side, keeping her body pressed close to the mare, gripping the reins. Once her feet hit the dirt, Sam gave a quick jerk on the reins. The mare wheeled around to face her and Sam felt a pulse of hope. She had Strawberry's attention.

"You're not going anywhere," she told the mare, as the heavy-headed stallion approached.

Neck arched, forelock tangled over his eyes, Hammer came at them, set on increasing his band.

"Back off," Sam shouted, but he was a wild thing, unafraid of human threats.

Strawberry lunged. Sam had wrapped the reins around her hands. She held on. A muscle binding her arm to her shoulder stretched.

Oh no. She must hang on, no matter what.

Hammer came on. From the ground, his chest looked as broad as the front of a car. She was all that stood between him and Strawberry. If he knocked her out of the way, his heavy hooves would trample her.

Strawberry dodged behind Sam and Hammer's attitude changed. His ears flattened. His head lowered, swinging side to side, flinging froth on the dry desert floor.

"Get back!" she shouted, but the blue stallion came on.

He'd decided she was the enemy.

Suddenly, Sam heard the thunder of hooves. She risked a look behind her and gasped.

The Phantom was galloping to Sam's rescue. Head high, mane floating like white flame, he carved a half circle around her. With the whirlwind of his passing, Sam knew the Phantom had marked her as his.

The explanation was hard to believe, but it was the only idea that made sense. He'd come running from the ridge before, blocking Hammer from stealing a single mare. This time, none of his mares were here. Only Sam.

In Hammer's eagerness to steal Strawberry, he'd forgotten to be watchful. His stride shortened at the sight of the other stallion. As he veered away from Sam, the Phantom flew after him.

Maybe Hammer couldn't bear the memory of his other humiliation. His hooves sprayed earth as he swung back with the agility of a cutting horse.

The blue roan stopped long enough to scream a challenge. He held a grudge against the silver stallion and this time he wouldn't run.

Sam wanted to throw rocks. She wanted to shout, to order her horse away from here. But the Phantom wasn't her horse anymore. His neigh pierced the quiet, returning Hammer's challenge. If the blue wanted a fight to the death, the Phantom would give it to him.

The stallions trotted forward. Their strides lengthened, flowing into a lope, a gallop. Then all grace fell away and they slammed together.

Please let him win. Please, if it's a fight to the death, let my horse live.